THE GHASTLY GHOST OF HILLBILLY HOLLOW

BLYTHE BAKER

DESCRIPTION

In Hillbilly Hollow, even the dead want the last word ...

When an eccentric local artist meets an untimely end during the annual Flower Festival, Emma gets pulled into two cases at once. First, the murder investigation. Second, the hunt for a dangerous burglar who has the whole town on edge.

After all-brawn-and-no-brains Sheriff Tucker declares the death an accident, Emma's search for the killer hits a dead end ... until a vengeful ghost comes calling. Can Emma decipher the mad ramblings of the disgruntled spirit?

_____

CHAPTER 1

*T*here was always something special about summertime in Hillbilly Hollow. Lightning bugs danced in the glow of early evening, the smell of honeysuckle wafted through open windows, and the flowers were in full bloom. As I drove into town, I had the windows down in the old truck, and my sunglasses on. The sights and smells of a country summer filled my senses as the radio blared an old rock song and I sang along at the top of my lungs.

I'd been back in Hillbilly Hollow for several weeks, and was getting back into the rhythm of farm life, and enjoying being part of the community. There were still so many things I missed about New York, but I had forgotten how much fun I'd had growing up in a small town. The local ice cream shop had better ice cream than I'd ever had anywhere else. Main Street was always festooned with lights and garlands at Christmastime, and everyone always rallied around the local sports teams to support the local kids. There were so many things I had taken for granted when I was young, before wanderlust pulled me away to the bright lights of the big city.

When I got to Main Street, signs were hanging from the

lampposts announcing the upcoming Hillbilly Hollow Flower Festival.

Grandpa had asked me to pick up chicken feed and some building supplies while I ran errands in town. I didn't mind running to town for this or that, or to see my friends. The distance between our farm and town had seemed like it took forever when I first got home. Now, I went to town almost every day. After all, a girl can only spend so much time on the farm with her grandparents before she starts to go a bit stir crazy.

The streets were a little busier than usual, with tourists starting to trickle in for the start of the Flower Festival. The local hotel, The Hollow Inn, was over a hundred years old, and a stagecoach stop had stood on that site before it. There was still a little restaurant on the first floor of the hotel which served breakfast and lunch. During the summer when there were lots of tourists in town for festivals and for Old Fort Days, the hotel was always full. Further out, an entrepreneurial family from St. Louis, the Shaffers, had bought the old Stephenson farm and converted it to a bed and breakfast, putting six little cottages on the property in addition to the huge, old farmhouse. The property had been featured in the Missouri tourist guide the year before and had gotten more popular since, often booking up solid in the summer.

The local feed and supply store, Farm King, was at the far end of Main Street, past the church and the walk-in clinic. Before I got that far, though, I decided I deserved to treat myself to a strawberry slush on such a beautiful summer day, so I stopped at Chapman's, the largest and newest gas station and convenience store Hillbilly Hollow had to offer.

Donna Selby was the daytime cashier at Chapman's. Her cousin Sherrie was in my class in school but Donna was a good five or six years younger, so I didn't know her as well growing up. I walked back to the slush machine and helped myself to a medium strawberry-flavored drink. Walking back up front, I took too eager a sip from the oversized straw and got brain freeze. Billy had taught me the trick of sticking my thumb against the roof of my mouth to warm up my palate. He was always full of obscure little tidbits of information like that. Being friends with the town doctor definitely had its perks.

As I got to the counter, there were a few people hanging around talking to Donna. I recognized Jasper Jenkins. His wife Ethel was one of Grandma's quilting circle friends. Lyndon Lowery was there too. He was one of the most successful farmers and land owners in town. Ted Baxter leaned on the counter across from Donna as well. He had been in our class, and Suzy told me that they had dated for a while before she reconnected with Brian, her now-fiancé. He was a nice-looking guy with blondish-brown hair and bright green eyes. Brian was more put-together, though, and his good looks were more polished. The more time I spent with Brian and Suzy together, the happier I was for her. He was a genuinely good guy, and really seemed to be in love with Suzy.

"Hello, Mr. Lowery, Mr. Jenkins. Hi, Ted. Everything alright?" I asked as I set my slush cup on the counter and put down a five-dollar bill.

"Hi, Emma," Ted said. "I guess you haven't heard, then?"

"Heard what?" I asked.

"This place was robbed last night," Mr. Lowery said in a hushed voice. "At gunpoint no less!"

"Oh, sugar! Is everyone okay?" I asked.

"Yeah, Caleb was working. Said a masked guy came right in, covered head to toe in black clothes, had a gun and a note that said 'empty the register'. He put the money in a sack and then ran out. Got away before Caleb could call the sheriff," Donna said, shaking her head. "Darn scary if you ask me."

"Probably one of these strangers in town," Mr. Jenkins said. "You know, all these tourists in from all over...no telling who's coming and going, not to mention *why* they're lurking around!"

"Wow, that's awful. Well, I'm glad Caleb's okay," I said, taking my change from Donna. "You be safe, won't you?" I gave her a concerned smile. "See you all later."

I got in my truck and headed over to the Posh Closet to see Suzy.

"Morning, Suz," I said as I walked in the door.

"Hi, Emma!" she cheerfully called from the rack of clothes she was working on.

"Bathroom," I said, putting my slush on the counter as I walked to the back.

A few minutes later, I returned.

"So did you hear," I started to ask Suzy, who was, by then, sitting behind the counter on a little stool.

"Yes! Crazy, isn't it? You don't think about an *armed robbery* someplace like this, but I guess no place is safe anymore." She shrugged.

I picked up my drink to take a sip and it was noticeably lighter than it had been when I set it down. "Did you drink my slush?" I asked her.

"Not all of it." She smirked. "Come on, Emma! You didn't bring me one," she rolled her eyes. "You left me no choice."

"*Whatever* was I *thinking?*" I said dramatically. "I will try to do better in the future!" We both laughed. "So, are you taking any extra precautions due to the robbery?"

"I don't know...I'm not sure I'd know what I could do differently," she replied.

"Maybe you should ask Tucker for some tips," I suggested.

Suzy rolled her eyes. "Or one of his deputies. Bless Tuck-

4

er's heart. I'm not sure he'd be much help. When they were handing out looks and muscles, he must've gotten in the muscles line twice, and forgot he was supposed to get in the line for brains as well." We both giggled.

"Well, I'm sure you'll be alright anyway. After all, you close up by five or six most days." I looked at my watch. "Oh, look at the time. I've got a lot left to do – I'd better run."

I gave Suzy a hug around the neck.

"Text me later. Oh!" Suzy said, "Want to go to dinner later? We'll get Billy to come, too."

"Sounds good! See ya!" I waved as I walked out the door and hopped into my truck. As I put on my seatbelt, my phone buzzed. It was a text from Billy.

BILLY: Heard there was holdup at Chapman's. U coming 2 town?

I DECIDED to hop out of my truck and walk over to the clinic instead of replying. It was only a few doors down from Suzy's shop.

Lena, the receptionist, was several years younger than us. She was married to Danny Baxter, who had taken over as preacher of the local church after Preacher Jacob was murdered.

"Hi, Lena." I smiled at the pretty redhead when I walked in. There was no one in the waiting room. "Is Bil- I mean, Dr. Will in today?" I giggled. I knew he went by Dr. Will Stone, trying to craft a more grown-up image for himself now that he was a successful doctor, but he'd only ever be Billy to Suzy and me.

Lena laughed. "Yes, Emma. He's here. Nobody's in the office – you want to head back?"

"Thanks!" I walked around the desk and to the little office he kept in the back corner.

"Yes, I am coming to town, as a matter of fact," I said, leaning against his door. "Do you suspect me of secretly being the Armed Bandit of Hillbilly Hollow?" I asked, dramatically.

"Hi, Emma," he said, a megawatt smile flashing from his tanned face. "I wouldn't put it past you, ya know. I've seen what you're capable of, after all, and am convinced nothing scares you."

"Well, almost nothing," I said, plopping down in the chair opposite his desk, and looking around at the walls of his office. They were covered with thank you cards, photos, and drawings, presumably from grateful patients. "Why'd you ask if I'd be in town today?"

"I just wanted to be sure you knew about the robbery – knew to keep your eyes peeled, that's all." He shrugged.

"Are you worried about me?" I grinned. "I should be worried about you. I mean, don't you keep some pretty high-dose baby aspirin around here?"

"Ha! Yes, if someone wants to make a killing on tongue depressors and antibacterial cream, I'm definitely in danger of being a target! We don't keep much in the way of serious medicine, and what we do have is under lock and key. It's a pretty good system. That's the great thing about the clinic, though – mostly insurance and credit cards – very little cash business."

"While I'm thinking about it, Suzy asked me to come down for dinner later. She wanted to know if you'd come too," I said.

"Yeah! That would be great!" He furrowed his brow, and cleared his throat. "I mean, that sounds cool. Whatever."

"Okay, I'd better roll. Lots to do today. Talk to you later?" I said.

"Sounds good. Be safe out there, Emma," he said in that stern, doctor-ly voice he sometimes used. I found it both extremely sweet and unbelievably dorky at the same time.

"Don't worry, I will!" I said, plucking a sucker from the jar on his desk as I left.

As I walked out to my truck, I pulled the wrapper from the sucker and stuffed the plastic into my pocket. I put the red disc against my tongue. *Mm. Strawberry!*

I heard a loud noise and my attention was pulled to the street. There were two motorcycles rolling up Main Street toward the diner. The motorcycles didn't look new – in fact, one of them looked pretty beaten up. The riders each wore a leather vest over their t-shirt and jeans, and each sported a very expensive-looking helmet. The look was a bit outdated, I thought, not to mention that it was far too hot for leather by the time the Flower Festival rolled around.

I wondered if the two bikers might be taking the scenic route from Springfield to St. Louis along old Route 66, and just stopping in town for a bite to eat. We sometimes got tourists who got off the old tourist route and came through to check out the town. It was good for business, I knew, and with so many friends and neighbors who had businesses of their own, I tried to be supportive.

Still, it was a reminder of how many newcomers we had coming through town lately, especially because of the Festival. I thought briefly of the recent robbery and wondered if a stranger was responsible or someone from right here in the Hollow.

CHAPTER 2

I stopped at Farm King and picked up the feed for the chickens, and also picked up a couple pairs of work pants for myself. I had already ruined one pair of good jeans with barbed wire and manure, and I was determined not to lose any more of my wardrobe to farm life. Even if I was going to stick around a while, there was no point in doing farm chores in jeans that cost a hundred-fifty bucks a pair.

I also stopped at the hardware store and picked up some building materials that they had put back for Grandpa. Grandma wanted to box in the vegetable garden so the deer and rabbits didn't keep getting her vegetables. She canned fruit and vegetables, and made pickles according to the season. She put a lot of the canned goods up for us to eat, but also donated some to various fundraisers throughout the year. Her sweet pickle recipe was so good, I hesitated to eat sweet pickles made by anyone else.

The guy behind the register was younger than me, and I didn't know him well. He called for someone from the back to help me get the supplies into the truck. Before long, I was loaded up and ready to check another errand off my list.

My next stop was the Hillbilly Hollow Museum. I had to drop off some fliers from the Historical Society and wanted to give some of my business cards to Jackie Colton, Suzy's Mom who was also the museum curator. I thought she might be willing to refer anyone to me who might need graphic design work. I had known Mrs. Colton my whole life, and she had always been a supporter of my graphic design work. I knew I would find the most volume of work online, but thought it would be gratifying if I could pick up a little local business as well.

My hands were full with two big boxes of fliers for Old Fort Days as I went into the museum. I balanced the boxes cautiously as I gingerly opened the door with the tips of my fingers. As I started through the door, someone pushed past me, nearly knocking me over.

There was no mistaking her wild, silver-white mane of hair, and the multi-colored tunic she wore. It was Melody Campbell, the popular local artist. There were several pieces of her work on permanent display at the museum.

"Really, do you have to be just where I'm trying to walk? Move aside! Honestly!" She made a tsk-tsk noise against her teeth with her tongue and shook her head as she pushed me aside.

She was known for her eccentricity as much as her highly sought after paintings. Her style was a mix of impressionism and cubism, marked by bold colors and subtle design. I didn't think her work was as good as many people did, but I had been lucky enough to visit lots of museums and local galleries in New York, so I considered myself pretty spoiled in that regard.

"Hi, Ms. Campbell," I said cautiously. "Everything alright?"

"Oh, yes, it's just wonderful!" she said, rolling her eyes exaggeratedly. "My car's in the shop, and I have to walk *all the way* back to my house with *all of this*," she said, holding up two large bags of art supplies. "So yes, Emma, it's just a *wonderful* day!" She started to huff off.

"Ms. Campbell, if you'll wait for…" I started to offer to drop her at her home if she'd wait for me to leave the fliers with Mrs. Colton.

"No, I will not wait! I've told you I'm very busy. Good day!" She stormed off.

Hmpf! Rude, much? I couldn't believe I was thinking of helping that cranky woman.

I spent a few minutes with Mrs. Colton, then ran over to Founders Park. The front entrance to Founders Park was two blocks behind the Historical Society. The park was also accessible through Hollow Heights Garden via an entrance on County Road 47 at the back. It had a small playground, several benches, and a large open area that was used for festivals. Hollow Heights Garden, though, was the highlight of the park, and a source of many visitors to Hillbilly Hollow each year. It was a beautifully landscaped space, rich with examples of local flowers and plants.

Each year, the kickoff of the Flower Festival was a charity auction held on the park grounds. Local artists, both professional and amateur, created beautiful themed banners to be sold in the auction. I had promised Grandma I'd buy a pretty banner for her to hang on the front porch. She had always wanted one, but never seemed to be able to win the ones she was after at the auction.

I stopped at the registration table to pick up an auction paddle, and had just enough time to make a quick run through of the items up for sale. There were a couple of pretty banners that I thought Grandma would like. There were several nice ones with scenes of our little downtown area, and some of the natural beauty spots from around the county. Several depicted the old fort here in town, same as it stood in modern day, while others showed scenes of it in its military heyday. I came upon one banner that had pretty colors, but the abstract style wasn't my taste. I thought I recognized it as Melody Campbell's work.

As I stood, looking over the piece, someone I had yet to run into since I'd been back in town was suddenly standing beside me.

"Well, if it isn't little Emma Hooper," the tall, perfectly coiffured blonde said from behind oversized black sunglasses.

"Hello, Lisa," I replied, trying to hold back the venom in my voice. All through school, Lisa Teller, now Lisa Teller-Parks, had always seemed to get the better of me. She ended up marrying Jason Parks, local realtor, but I'd heard that they had recently gotten divorced.

She and I ended up in competition for everything. From class secretary to cheerleading – whatever I went out for, she did too, and she usually beat me. Things got really bad between us our senior year of high school. She had developed a crush on Billy, and everyone knew we were close. Apparently she was flirting with Billy, who wasn't interested, and when he rejected her, she started a hurtful rumor about us. She had told everyone in school that Billy's parents were broke, and weren't telling him, but were about to lose their house. She said that was why we were close, Broke Billy and Little Orphan Emma. Even though none of it was true, and we'd all grown up, seeing her made my blood boil.

"I see you're looking at the Campbell banner. Looks like you finally developed decent taste after all these years. I mean, you wouldn't know it looking at your clothes." She smirked.

"You know, I hear you've made Jason a very happy man." I smiled at her.

"We're…divorced, actually," she replied, lifting her nose in the air.

"I know. That's what I meant. Enjoy the auction!" I giggled as I walked off to take my spot.

I didn't win the first banner I bid on. It was a pretty garden scene with hydrangeas all over it. Prudence Huffler was bidding on it, and I didn't have the heart to outbid her after all she'd been through with losing Preacher Jacob just a few months before. I couldn't say that Prudence looked happy, exactly, but she definitely looked better than she had during her darkest days.

The abstract banner came up, and Lisa immediately bid.

"Fifteen," she said, holding up her paddle nonchalantly.

Someone off to the side offered twenty.

"Twenty-five," I countered.

"Thirty," Lisa said.

"Thirty-five," I replied. Most of the banners had gone for between twenty and fifty dollars, so the auctioneer, Mayor Bigsby himself, was growing excited.

"Forty-five!" Lisa said authoritatively.

"Fifty!" I countered.

Another hand went up somewhere in the crowd, and Mayor Bigsby pointed, yelling, "Sixty," but never took his eyes off of Lisa and me. He had spent enough time at auctions to know a bidding war when he saw one.

"Seventy-five dollars!" Lisa shouted, holding her paddle high. The crowd grew quiet.

I chuckled. "One hundred dollars!" I replied. There was an audible gasp.

Mayor Bigsby looked at Lisa, who shook her head back and forth.

"Sold, to Emma Hooper for one hundred dollars! Emma, thank you for being such a generous supporter of the Historical Society!" Mayor Bigsby said.

I smiled and nodded graciously. *Well, crap!* I thought, *that wasn't even the banner I wanted, and I sure didn't mean to pay a hundred bucks for it!* I just hadn't wanted to see Lisa win.

I paid for my purchase and headed back toward the main entrance. The banner was more expensive than I had intended, but it was a pretty color combination, and would look nice hanging on our front porch. Besides, the money did go to a good cause and Grandma would just be happy to have a piece of artwork of her very own.

As I started walking back to the truck with my purchase, Jerry Langston, the local veterinarian, chased me down. "Emma! Emma!" he said, as he jogged up to meet me.

"Hi, Dr. Langston. Everything okay?" I asked.

"Yes, yes!" he snapped impatiently. "I need that banner." He dug into his pocket and retrieved his wallet, opening it and digging through the cash inside. "How much did you pay for it?" he asked.

"Excuse me?" I asked incredulously.

"You heard me. How much did you *pay* for it?" He pulled a few twenties from the wallet.

"Dr. Langston, this is mine, I…" I started to protest, and he cut me off.

"*Hmpf!* Alright, then! I'll give you twenty over the asking price and not a penny more! Here!" He shoved a handful of bills at me, and went to grab the banner.

I was incensed! The banner was hideous, true enough, but the colors were nice, and there was something strangely familiar about it. Almost comforting in a way I couldn't explain. It was for my grandma, and there was no way I was going to let someone take it from me.

"No, sir!" I pushed back on his fistful of cash. "This is for my grandma, and I'm taking it home to her now. Good day, Dr. Langston."

I pushed past him and headed toward my truck. I could've sworn I heard an almost growling sound as I walked away.

As I drove home, I couldn't help but wonder again about the robbery that was the talk of the town. Hillbilly Hollow wasn't that close to the interstate. It was the type of place you had to make an effort to come visit. I couldn't believe some random criminal would go out of their way to come to our little town to rob a gas station. At the same time, if it wasn't a stranger, it had to be someone local. There were a few unsavory characters that hung out at Happy Hills, the trailer park out past the junkyard on the far outskirts of town. Still, I couldn't imagine anyone being so brazen as to risk being seen and caught.

I wondered if the robbery had everyone else in town on edge too. Lisa had been in rare form today, even for her. I felt a twinge of regret at making fun of her divorce, but after all, she had been really hateful to Billy and me when we were kids, so maybe she deserved it. Melody Campbell had shocked me with her rudeness too, and for no apparent reason. I should've probably chased her down to make her let me drive her home. She lived a good distance out at the edge of town, and she wasn't a young woman anymore. Still, you can't help someone who doesn't want to be helped, I supposed.

Dr. Langston was another piece of work. I couldn't think why in the world he would expect me to give up the banner I had *just* bid to win. Of course, he clearly didn't know how much I had overpaid for it, but still, it was rude of him to try to take it from me so forcefully.

The Flower Festival was supposed to be a fun time – one

of the best weeks to be in Hillbilly Hollow. This year felt different, though. I wasn't sure if it was the fog of Preacher Jacob's death a few months before, or something else, but it was as if there was something in the air in Hillbilly Hollow. Whatever it was, I didn't like it one bit.

CHAPTER 3

*W*hen I got home, my shadow was waiting for me on the back porch.

"Hi, Snowball," I said as I walked around and opened the back gate of the pickup. I reached down, scratching the little goat under the chin. True, kittens were adorable and dogs were man's best friend, but if this little nanny goat had taken it upon herself to adopt me, who was I to stop her? Besides, I'd grown attached to the silly girl. "Come on, let's take these down to the shed."

I grabbed the bags from the hardware store and headed down to the equipment shed to retrieve a wheelbarrow. Snowball followed along behind me. I grabbed the green wheelbarrow, the one with the best tires, and pulled it out, parking it outside as I closed the shed doors. I turned to push it to the truck, only to find that Snowball was sitting in it.

"What do you think you're doing?" I asked, hands on hips. She bleated in reply. I lifted the barrel, and she cocked her head up, enjoying the view. "Now I know what Cleopatra's litter-bearers felt like carrying her around!" I chuckled.

I tipped the wheelbarrow up, causing Snowball to hop

out, loaded the feed into it, and headed to the chicken coop. I put the feed in the bin attached to the outside of the coop and secured it closed, then returned the wheelbarrow to the shed and headed into the house feeling very accomplished.

"Hi, Grandma," I said, kissing her cheek as I walked in. She and Grandpa were at the kitchen table, eating lunch.

"Emma, dear! There's some cold chicken in the fridge, if you're hungry," she said, smiling up at me. Grandpa was tucking into a drumstick. I grabbed a plate and joined them.

"Did you hear about the robbery?" I asked as I took a bite of potato salad.

"Oh, yes!" Grandma replied. "Just terrible! I'm glad that Gentry boy wasn't hurt. Caleb, I think his name is."

"Shame. Person can't even go to the market without having to worry about some crazy person anymore," Grandpa said, shaking his head. "Don't know what the world's a-comin' to!"

"Yeah, I ran into Mr. Jenkins – Jasper that is – in the market. He and Mr. Lowery seem to think it's someone from outside of town – maybe just passing through," I added.

"Well, they're long gone if Tucker's on the case, that's for sure!" Grandma chuckled.

I decided to steer the conversation to a more upbeat topic. "So Grandpa," I said taking a big gulp of lemonade, "Did you think any more about my proposal? About the satellite?" I asked cautiously.

I wanted him to agree to let me get satellite service so I could have internet at the house. If I was going to stay in Hillbilly Hollow, for a while at least, I needed access to the internet so I could work. I had given up my graphic design job with a firm in New York after I'd been hit by a taxi. I came home to rest and recuperate, which Dr. Jenson, my therapist, had recommended. He was sure the *spirits* I was seeing were a byproduct of electrical impulses in my brain thanks to the injury I sustained. I wasn't so sure. I could continue to pick up some graphic design work if I had reliable internet service. Otherwise, I'd have to go to the library or coffee shop in town, and rely on Wi-Fi.

"Hmm," Grandpa said, scratching his chin. I could hear his rough fingers drag across his stubble from not having shaved that morning. "I don't know, Emma. Not much on all that new-fangled technology."

"I know, Grandpa, but just hear me out. If I get internet service, I can include all the TV channels for you and Grandma. You can watch whatever you want, anytime!" I smiled at Grandma.

"Already got six channels. Don't see much need for more." He shook his head and took another bite of chicken.

"Well," I mustered up my best sales pitch. "Did you know that there's a channel just dedicated to farm reports? All the commodities pricing is there, and you can get to the almanac right from the remote. There's also a channel that plays nothing but game shows! You like those. And Grandma," I looked at her, "there's a channel that has old TV shows. You can watch your favorites every day, if you want!"

"Oh, I do like that," she replied enthusiastically.

"Won't cost me anything?" Grandpa asked.

"No, Grandpa." I was happy to foot the bill, though I was pretty sure that they had more zeroes in their bank balance than I'd ever see in my lifetime.

"Alright then," he replied quietly, and took a sip of lemonade.

"Thanks, Grandpa!"

"Suppose this means you're sticking around a bit, then," he said.

"I think I am...if that's okay with you two?" I replied hesitantly.

"Good!" I was shocked at his enthusiastic reply. "I mean,

there's a lot of work around here. I can do it on my own just fine, but easier with one more."

He got up and left the table. Grandma patted me on the hand.

* * *

GRANDMA HAD SOAKED some sheets and put them up in front of the windows to cool the house down. She always called it nature's air conditioning. The breeze passing through the open windows made the water in the sheets evaporate, and cooled the house down in the heat of the afternoon.

I remembered that I had left the banner in the cab of the truck and retrieved it.

Grandma was thrilled. "Oh, I just love the colors! And the style...it's so...it's just so *artistic!*" she said.

Funnily enough, I knew what she meant. We hung it on the front porch, fussing with the placement until she was perfectly happy with it. I asked Grandma to stand beside the banner so I could snap a photo with my phone. She did so proudly, happy to own a piece of authentic local art.

I went to take a bath and get cleaned up. I planned on stopping in the general store before I met Suzy and Billy for dinner, to ask about the satellite service. That was one convenient thing about a small town. The general store sold absolutely everything, and if they didn't have it, they could get it.

I had put some bath salts in the water, and slathered my face with a mud mask. It wasn't much of a luxury, but it was as close as I could get to a spa day on the farm. Since I'd been home, my muscles had gotten more accustomed to doing farm chores, but I still experienced some soreness here and there.

Snowball was on the floor near the washing machine, relaxing. I put my head back and tried to relax while the mud mask worked its magic. I heard a little rustle at the side of the tub, and put my hand down to soothe Snowball. Instead, my palm connected with something sharp, and I drew it back quickly.

"Sugar!" I exclaimed, grabbing my hand as I put myself upright in the tub, water sloshing everywhere. I looked down to find Martha Washington and Grace Coolidge, two of Grandma's hens, looking up at me, the little troublemakers. My hand was bleeding a little, and I wasn't sure if it was from a scratch or peck with their beaks.

I used the washcloth to remove the mud mask with my undamaged hand, and got out of the tub, shooing the chickens out of the laundry room. I rinsed my hand under the sink, and poured alcohol on the open wound before putting a bandage over it. I'd have to let Billy take a look.

It was still hot outside, so I put on a sundress and a pair of flats, kissed Grandma goodnight and headed out to get in the truck. I thought I had better text Billy.

ME: Can u meet me at the clinic?
    BILLY: Sure. U ok?
    ME: Chicken – 1 me – 0

HE SENT BACK an emoji that was laughing with tears coming out of its eyes.

I met Billy at the clinic a few minutes later. He unlocked the door and showed me into the exam room.

"So, a chicken injury, this time?" he asked, flipping on the bright fluorescent light overhead. "I'm glad to see you've moved on from goats. Variety is the spice of life, after all." He winked at me as I hopped up onto the exam table, and presented my outstretched palm.

"I was in the tub, and heard a noise, and when I put my hand down, one of them got me. Either Martha or Grace, I'm not sure which," I said.

"Martha or Grace?" he asked, pulling off the bandage.

"Martha Washington or Grace Coolidge," I replied as if it were a perfectly normal thing to say.

"Oh, of course. I do love your Grandma, by the way. Who else gives each chicken a name, let alone such a regal one?" He squinted a little as he looked at my palm. "Hold still," he said, reaching for a squeeze bottle behind him with a goose-neck. He squirted some sort of antiseptic, and blotted it with a clean piece of gauze.

"It doesn't look too deep. I don't think you need stitches. But...have you had a tetanus shot lately?" He raised an eyebrow, doing that intimidating doctor face.

"Um... in school, maybe? I've no idea." I shrugged.

"Hmm. Well, we should probably give you one just in case. Be right back." He returned a moment later with a small syringe. He grabbed an alcohol wipe and stood to face me. "Left or right?" he asked.

"Left or right what?" I replied, concerned about where he was thinking of putting that needle.

Billy threw his head back and laughed with his whole body. "Left or right *shoulder*, Emma!"

"Oh," I replied, blushing. "Okay. Left, I guess."

He walked around to my left side. The sundress I had worn was cut in a little at the shoulder, which was convenient for the purpose. Billy put his left hand on the skin of my left shoulder, and applied the alcohol swab. A shiver ran through me and I got goosebumps.

"You okay?" he asked before proceeding.

"Yeah, of course. Just someone walking across my grave."

I gave a nervous chuckle.

"Okay, little stick. Here we go." Billy was a big guy, and his hands matched his stature. He held my shoulder firmly as he jabbed me with the needle.

"*Yowch!*" I exclaimed as he pushed in the plunger, shooting the medicine into my bloodstream.

Billy chuckled as he tossed the needle into a safety container. "Come on now, it's not that bad, is it?"

He wiped the injection site with another alcohol swab, and opened a bandage, adhering it to the spot. "Now, Lena's daughter, Madison, makes me kiss the spot on her arm where I put the bandage after I give her a shot." He chuckled a bit nervously, and rubbed my shoulder where he'd put the bandage. I chuckled too, and felt my cheeks turning pink.

He had been my best friend when we were kids, but he definitely wasn't a kid anymore. If my friends in New York had run into someone as tall, dark, and handsome as him, they'd have eaten him alive. I might have too, for that matter, but *this* wasn't some random, handsome stranger. This was Billy Stone. *My* Billy Stone. It all felt very...complicated.

"Thanks," I said quietly. "It wasn't too bad. We should probably go over to meet Suzy, don't you think?"

"Yeah, I'm pretty hungry," he replied.

* * *

WE MET Suzy at the diner. She had a table when we got there, and waved when she saw us walk in the door.

"Hi Emma and Billy...boy, doesn't that just roll off the tongue?" She laughed, then exclaimed, "Ow!"

"Oh, was that you, Suzy? Sorry about that. I thought I was kicking the table." Billy smirked. "My big feet always get in the way." They exchanged a look.

"They look really busy here tonight," I said. "Maybe we should've gone to Chez Jose instead?"

"Sherrie said she'll be here in a minute. Somebody went home sick, or something," Suzy replied.

A few minutes later, Sherrie Selby, a girl we knew from school, came over to take our order. "Hi," she said, seeming out of breath. "If you guys need a minute, I can come back, but it'll be faster if I take your whole order at once." She wiped the back of her hand across her brow.

"I think we can order now," Suzy said.

Billy and I looked at each other and mouthed the word, 'bossy!'

"Why is it so packed, Sherrie?" I asked.

"Well, Jennie – Jennie Weaver – she had to leave early. She was real upset," Sherrie said, whispering the last part as she leaned over the table.

"What happened?" Suzy immediately leaned in and asked.

"Well," Sherrie looked around, then leaned in again, "you didn't get it from me, but Melody Campbell was in here at lunch and complained to Cooper over there that Jennie was rude and gave her the wrong food. She told Cooper she thought he should fire Jennie. Can you believe that? You're gonna try to take somebody's job cause they're having an off day?" She shook her head. "Anyway, that boyfriend of Jennie's came and picked her up because she was too upset to work the dinner shift." She shrugged and looked over her shoulder. "So, do you guys wanna go ahead and order?"

She took our orders and Suzy ordered for her fiancé, Brian, who was on his way to join us.

We sat there, chatting for a few minutes before Brian arrived. Sherrie had just put our plates down in front of us when Billy got a call. "This is Dr. Will," he answered. He always answered that way when there was no caller ID. Suzy and I both stifled giggles.

"Hey Tucker. Oh no! Yeah, okay…yeah…I can be there soon. I'm on my way," Billy said, hanging up the phone.

"Everything okay?" Brian asked him.

"No, I'm afraid not. There's been some sort of accident out on the highway at the south edge of town. Looks like a pedestrian was hit." He shook his head, and I winced, drawing my hand up to my mouth.

"That's awful!" I said.

"Terrible! Suzy added.

"Emma, would you mind boxing my food up and dropping it at my house, and maybe let Halee out to do her business?" He dropped the key to his house on the table with a twenty to cover dinner.

"Sure, of course. Go do what you need to do, I'll take care of it," I said.

I finished dinner with Suzy and Brian and headed over to Billy's with his dinner all boxed up to-go. I'd been at his house a few times since I'd been back in town, and still thought it was one of the most beautiful houses I'd ever seen.

As soon as I walked in the door, Halee came running. She was a chocolate brown malti-poo with the sweetest little brown eyes. I absolutely adored her, and from the way her little tail wagged when she saw me, the feeling was mutual.

I put Billy's food in the fridge, and took Halee into the backyard to let her do her business. I sat out there for a few minutes, on the edge of the deck with my feet in the grass of the backyard. It was a beautiful evening. Then I realized that for someone, it wasn't. For whoever Billy went to go take care of, it might be a life-changing evening, or worse.

CHAPTER 4

I had given Halee a final scratch behind the ear, and was about to leave when I heard the front door open and shut.

"Hi…I'm surprised you're still here," Billy said as he walked in, looking beat.

"Oh, I didn't mean to be. I was sitting in the back, playing with Halee and time got away from me." I looked down at my watch and it was just after eight. Billy had left the diner a little after five. "Are you okay?" I asked him tentatively.

"Yeah, I'm okay." Billy rubbed his palm up and down the back of his neck as he put his bag in a chair in the living room.

"You look tired. I'll head out –let you get some rest," I said, putting his house key on the coffee table. "Goodnight, Billy," I said.

He grabbed my arm as I walked by him and hugged me. "Could you stay just a little while? Just while I eat dinner, maybe?" he asked.

"Of course," I replied. "One for all…"

"And all for one," he finished. He gave me a little smile.

27

"Here, sit down," I said, gesturing toward the sofa as I threw my purse into the chair beside his bag. "I'll grab your food. It's in the fridge."

I brought him the to-go container and a soda. He wolfed down the cold burger and fries like he hadn't had food in days. I sat on the other end of the sofa from him, careful not to get too close, lest I get in the way of his ravenous eating and get bitten. After taking a few bites, and chugging on the drink, he finally stopped long enough to speak.

"It was Melody Campbell," he said, wiping the corner of his mouth with the back of his hand. "She was in the ditch… hit by a car." He shook his head as he said it, and his eyes went dark.

"Oh, no! Is she…?" I asked.

"Yeah, I'm afraid so." He shook his head again. "Emma, it was bad. Really bad."

"What in the world happened?" I asked.

"She was on the main highway out of town – must've been walking home," he replied.

"Oh, you know what?" I suddenly remembered my earlier conversation with her. "Billy, I saw her this afternoon…at the museum. She said her car was in the shop. I was going to offer to drop her off but she was so rude, she wouldn't even slow down to listen to me, so I dropped it."

I drew both hands to my mouth and gasped. "Oh, Billy! If I had only made her listen…if I had given her a ride…I feel terrible!" My eyes started to well up a little.

Billy put down the box of food, and put an arm around me. "Shh, Emma, no. Stop it. It wasn't your fault. You can't think that. You said you tried to help her and she wouldn't listen. You know that's not your fault."

His words made me feel better. He had always known just what to say to comfort me. "Thanks, Billy," I said, patting his hand gently, indicating he could go back to his burger, which he did immediately. "I just can't believe a hit-and-run. First a robbery, now this. It's crazy!"

"Yeah, that's what *Tucker* said, anyway." Billy shook his head, emphasizing the name.

"What does that mean?" I asked.

"Well, he's convinced it was just a hit-and-run accident," Billy said. "But I'm not so sure."

"What do you think happened?" I asked.

"I don't know, Emma," he replied. "I didn't see any brake marks, and examining the body, I'm certain the car never even slowed down. I have to think…I don't know…it was like someone was *trying* to hit her."

"Really?" I replied. "That's awful! It's hard to imagine someone could do that. Although, I mean, not to talk ill of the dead, but she wasn't always the easiest person to deal with." I shrugged.

"I know. I heard that she and her sister didn't get along very well. You know, Cadence? She's the groundskeeper over at the cemetery. She's a bit of an odd bird too." He raised an eyebrow knowingly.

Billy pushed the food container back away from the edge of the coffee table, where Halee was investigating the smells emanating from it. She hopped up on the sofa between us, stretching out on her back so her front paws were on my leg, and her back paws were on Billy's, as if demanding we both pet her at the same time.

I gave Halee's belly a little rub, and stood up to leave. "It's late, I'd better go. Grandpa has me on pig duty tomorrow morning." I rolled my eyes playfully, and grinned.

"Thanks for coming to check on Halee." Billy smiled at me.

"Get some sleep, Billy," I said as I opened the front door. "Goodnight."

* * *

WHEN I GOT BACK to the farm I changed into my sleep shorts and t-shirt, and slipped on my muck boots to visit the outhouse before bed. Snowball ambled along behind me and made herself comfy in a grassy spot at the edge of the woods while she waited for me. I took care of business, and stepped back out into the warm evening air. I called for Snowball, and she walked over to me cautiously, then leaned to the side as if looking behind me.

"What's wrong, girl?" I asked, putting my hands on my knees and bending toward her.

She looked at me, bleated, and crooked her head to the side again.

"What is it, Snowball?"

"Good grief! Turn around already!" I heard a faraway voice say behind me.

I spun on my heel, and gasped in surprise. An apparition was standing before me, silvery-white hair standing wildly on end, with the bright colors of her tunic muted against her ethereal form.

"Melody Campbell?" I asked.

"No, it's Marilyn Monroe! Of course it's me!" she said, putting her ghostly hands on the hips of her semi-transparent form.

"What – what are you doing here?" I asked. I hadn't seen any visions, or spirits, or whatever they were for just long enough that I thought it might be over.

"Well, I'm here to see you, of course! Honestly! Not much of a thinker, are you?" the spirit version of Melody replied.

"Ms. Campbell," I said, blinking to be sure I was truly awake and not just dreaming. "I'm not even sure why I can see you, let alone what I can do for you."

"Well, you seem to be the only one who can see me, and I

30

can't rest until whoever killed me is brought to justice, so…" She opened her eyes wide and turned her palms up in a lifting motion, as if her meaning was obvious.

"So…what, then?" I replied.

"So…you're up! Good grief, you aren't the chippiest cookie in the bag, are ya?"

"Look, Tucker said it was a freak accident," I objected.

"Are you kiddin' me? That moron couldn't recognize a crime if he saw it happening! They swerved to hit me. It happened so fast I couldn't see who was driving. I need *you*, Emma. You're the only one that can see me." She was growing impatient.

"I can definitely see you…why can I hear you, though? When I've…I mean, the last time I had…I've never had a ghost talk to me before." When I had seen spirits before, they had never spoken.

"Well, let me explain it all, because I'm an expert, what with having been dead for about six hours and all." She gave an exaggerated head roll. "How should I know? Maybe because you were the last person I talked to? Not like somebody showed up to give me a manual on how to be a ghost. Honestly!"

"Look, I'm sorry, but I don't think I can help you, and I'm very tired, so float off and find somebody else. Maybe a cop or a detective or somebody – I'm neither. Goodnight!"

I looked down at Snowball, who was lying in a grassy spot watching the exchange disinterestedly. "Come on, Snowball!"

The little goat hopped up and followed me into the house. Once upstairs in my attic room, I kicked off my boots and flopped onto my bed.

* * *

I WAS TRYING to doze off, when I heard the hangers on the clothing rack I used as a makeshift closet start to clatter together. I cracked open my eye and looked over to find Melody standing between the rack and my bed.

"What are you *doing* in here?" I said. "I told you I can't do anything for you!"

"I need you, Emma! You're the only one who can help me!" she said, seeming even more annoyed.

"I told you, there's nothing I can do – I don't know anything about investigating a murder. *If* you really were murdered," I replied.

"I heard you helped figure out what had happened to Preacher Jacob. I heard that *you* stuck your nose in, and caught Teller at the scene of the crime!" She stood, or hovered, by the bed.

"I wouldn't have any idea what to do." I resisted. I was getting into a good flow at the farm and would be doing some remote design work as well. I wasn't sure I had the time, let alone the inclination, for amateur sleuthing.

"I'll haunt you until you agree to help, ya know. It might be hard to believe, but I can be very annoying when I wanna be," she said.

"You don't say," I replied, rolling my eyes.

"Emmaaaaaaaa Hoooooooperrrrrrr," she moaned, putting her arms out exaggerated in front of her. "Aveeeeenge meeeeee....oooooooooooh!"

"What are you doing?" I asked.

"I'm moaning. Isn't that what ghosts are supposed to do? Oooooooh!"

I let out a heavy sigh. "Okay. Okay! I'll see what I can do."

"Well, it's about time!" she said, putting her hands on her hips. "Go to the scene of the crime, Emma. There has to be proof someone was gunning for me. It wasn't an accident."

Her spectral form floated down to the far end of the attic.

As she was in front of the window on the far end of the room, she turned back.

"Thank you for helping me, Emma," she said quickly, then turned, and disappeared through the wall.

I lay back in my bed and tucked my hands under my head. I'd have to see if I could tell anything from the accident scene in the morning. I might try talking to Tucker and see if there was any more information that Billy didn't already share with me. I knew if I wanted to get Melody out of my house, and out of my head, I'd have to see if I could figure out what really happened.

CHAPTER 5

I got up extra early the next day – even before Grandma and Grandpa.

I grabbed a flashlight from the kitchen drawer and headed off down the highway toward Melody's house. I saw the yellow police caution tape in the brush on the side of the road, and knew I'd found the scene of the accident...or crime, according to Melody.

I pulled the truck along the side of the road, just beyond the last piece of plastic tape, the loose end of which was dancing along in a light gust of summer breeze. I walked back toward the spot where Melody had been killed. I saw the tire tracks emerging from the grassy area in front of the woods on the side of the road. The grass was matted and dark where the tires had traveled from the grass, onto the gravel, and finally back up onto the pavement.

I shone the flashlight on the spot and moved it back and forth from the tire tracks, back to where our old farm truck was pulled alongside the road. I realized that the grass on either side of the greasy tire marks was tall and thick. It was only matted down to the width of the tires themselves. The muck boots I wore were about a foot tall, and the grass there alongside the road, including what was between the tire tracks, was almost to the tops of them. Further back, in the spot that I knew must have been where Melody met her demise, the grass was even higher.

Hmm, I thought. *If the grass wasn't bent over between the tire tracks, it must've been a pickup, not a car.*

I walked a little further along the road, beyond the piece of yellow tape that was on the side closest to town. I shone my flashlight up the road. The blacktop surface extended about a foot and a half beyond the white lines on the outside edge of the road. Beyond that was about a foot of large, heavy gravel, which tapered off into fine gravel and dust before transitioning to the tall grass beyond the edge of the road itself. I turned my light down the road toward town, and slowly scanned it from the pavement, to the gravel, to the grass.

The grassy area was pretty flat, parallel with the road surface for a couple of feet until it gradually dipped down into a ditch, the bottom of which was about ten feet from the edge of the pavement. As I looked at the grass, I realized that there was a path worn in the grass, parallel to the white line at the edge of the road. I followed the path, and it continued beyond the spot where the tire marks veered from the pavement to the grass, and up further along the road, as far as I walked.

A path along the road, I realized, *where someone was walking. Where Melody was walking before she was hit!*

From the location of the tire tracks, and how far along behind the worn path in the grass that they followed, I knew Melody was right. Whoever had hit her had veered off the road, well into the grassy area, following her path for a while before connecting with the poor woman, sending her into the ditch. I was certainly no forensic investigator, but to my untrained eye, it looked intentional.

First light was beginning to creep over the horizon. I waited for a few minutes for there to be enough light, then took some photos with my phone of the path where the grass had been trampled down, the tire marks cutting toward the grass, and the tire marks as they returned to the road.

With more light, I walked down closer to where Melody must've landed. I assumed that the sheriff's department, however incompetent they may be, picked up most of the evidence. When I looked around, the theory seemed to have been confirmed, since I didn't see any signs of Melody's belongings.

I walked along the edge of the woods, back toward the tire tracks that exited the grass. As I walked back up toward my truck, along the inside edge of the tire marks, a flash of something pale caught my eye among the green foliage.

I looked more closely and realized, it was a broken-off sapling with a streak of silvery-white paint along its bark on the side that faced the tire tracks. I took a photo of it, wondering if it could be paint from the truck that hit Melody.

I walked back to my truck. As I sat behind the wheel, it hit me that I might need some help figuring out who could've held enough of a grudge against Melody to want to kill her. If nothing else, it would be good to have someone to bounce ideas off of.

My mind immediately went to Billy. I knew, though, after the scuffle I'd recently gotten into with Mayor Teller over Preacher Jacob, that Billy would never stand for me snooping around. He had become very protective of me since I'd been back, and while I appreciated it, his protectiveness could hinder my ability to solve Melody's murder.

I could talk to Suzy. She knew everyone in town, she was great at reading people, and she was clever. Still, I had never told her about my visions. She might not take the idea that her best friend could see ghosts particularly well. I thought about it for a moment, then started the truck and headed toward town.

I stopped in Chapman's gas station to get a cup of coffee. As I waited for the person in front of me to pay for their donut and lottery scratcher, I scanned the boxes of impulse items on the counter. I looked to the far end and saw the tiny, rolled-up horoscope scrolls like the ones that Suzy and I used to love as little girls. We would pour over our horoscopes with a fine-toothed comb.

That's it! I thought. Suzy might not be able to take the idea of me being able to see ghosts, but she would definitely buy me having become psychic after my accident.

I went back across town to the sheriff's office. By the time I pulled into the sheriff's department parking lot, it was after six in the morning. I walked in and asked for Tucker. Deputy Johnson told me Tucker had just gotten in and asked me to wait a couple of minutes. I sat patiently in the lobby and sipped my coffee.

After a short wait, the deputy showed me back to see Tucker.

"Morning Emma," he said. "Everything alright?"

"Hi, Tucker. Yep, I'm fine, thanks!" I replied. "Listen…I was just driving out on the highway and passed by the spot where, well, you know – Melody?" I said.

"Yeah, darn shame about Melody," he replied, shaking his head. "Terrible accident."

"About that…something caught my eye in the sunlight as I drove by," I said, "so I stopped and had a look. When I got closer, I could see it was a sapling, and it looked like it had paint rubbed along it. Do you think that could be from the car? You know, like evidence?" I said the last part sheepishly, trying to put him more at ease to encourage his responsiveness to my questions.

"Oh, well, I dunno, Emma. I'm not sure a little smudge of paint would tell us anything about what kinda car it was," he sighed. "I honestly think it was just a hit-and-run freak accident. Probably somebody just passing through."

"Oh, okay," I said, standing up from my chair, which was across from his desk. "I just wondered if there was anyone who she didn't get along with. Maybe someone who even hated her enough to hurt her."

Tucker stood and walked around the desk toward me. He put a friendly arm around my shoulders, and I was a little taken aback by how muscular his arms were. I could only imagine a criminal trying to get away and being on the receiving end of the force of that much brawn.

"Now listen, Emma, don't you worry," he said. "The boys and I have got this thing under control. We're going to keep you and everyone else in Hillbilly Hollow safe. I can promise ya that." He gave me a reassuring smile. If I hadn't known that he was so goofy, I'd have had total confidence in his words and soothing manner.

"So, one other thing I meant to ask," I said as he ushered me toward the door. "This thing with Melody...it doesn't have anything to do with the robbery over at Chapman's, does it?"

"No, I don't think so," he said, running his thumb and forefinger across his thick, blonde beard. "I'm sure they're just two unrelated incidents. Now you have a good day, Emma. And like I said, don't worry." He pointed his finger at me for emphasis and gave me a confident nod.

Sweet Adeline's bakery was open by that time, and I popped in for a few donuts and texted Suzy.

ME: Can i swing by?
    SUZY: Only if u bring food
    ME: Already got it – heading ur way!

SUZY'S HOUSE WAS BEAUTIFUL, but not nearly as impressive as Billy's. Suzy lived a couple of blocks off of Main Street, near the park. Her house was a brick, three-bedroom crafter's cottage. I knocked on the front door and, seeing the donuts, Suzy immediately let me in.

"Morning, Emma! My new favorite person who comes bearing sugar!" She chuckled, walking into the kitchen and grabbing a plate from the cabinet on which to place the donuts. She picked up the plate and a cup of coffee and set them down on her breakfast nook table where her own cup of coffee already sat. "So, to what do I owe this very early morning visit?" she asked, tucking into her favorite donut flavor, old fashioned with chocolate frosting.

"Well, you heard about Melody Campbell, right?" I asked.

"Oh, yeah! I heard last night! It's awful," she replied, taking a sip of coffee.

"I just drove by the spot...you know, where it happened?" I replied. "And... there's something else – something I've been wanting to tell you for a while, but I wasn't sure how."

She leaned forward and grabbed my hand. "Emma, I'm your best friend! You can tell me *anything*, you know that!" Her tone was serious but supportive.

"Well, you know how some people are...I guess you'd call it *sensitive* to things like, knowing what's going to happen, or sensing people from beyond the grave?" I was trying to be equal parts dramatic, to keep her interest, and believable.

"Sure! I keep hoping that I'll develop a psychic connection to the state lottery drawing, but it hasn't happened yet." She giggled.

"Well, sometimes, people report having strange experiences after a bad accident. You know, like the one I had in New York right before I moved back." I scanned her face, trying to gauge her expression. She looked curious, but her face seemed open. "That's what happened to me, Suzy. So now, I have this sort of connection to – I don't know what – the other side?"

Suzy grinned a little. "Emma, are you being straight with me? You're not putting me on, are you?" she asked.

"Absolutely not! I'm telling the truth!" I nodded.

"Well..." she paused for an interminable moment. "That sounds kind of freaky, but if anyone would get a bizarre, head-bump-related superpower, it would be you!" She gave a full laugh, and I laughed a little too.

"So, Melody having died...something has been nagging at me about it. Suzy, I think she was murdered," I said.

Suzy gasped. "Murdered? Really? Who in the world?" She seemed surprised, but not to the point of being unreasonable.

"I need someone to help me with figuring out what happened to her. I have a feeling her soul isn't at rest and won't be until we find her killer," I said. I had guessed that explaining my experiences as being 'psychic' and a vague feeling that Melody's soul wasn't at rest would be more palatable than saying I saw ghosts on the farm, which was the whole truth.

"Wow, okay..." she said, and I knew she was considering what I had told her. "So, who do you think might have done it?"

I reminded Suzy that Jennie Weaver had been so upset at Melody's criticism of her waitressing skills that she – or her unsavory boyfriend – might be to blame. I told her I wasn't sure who else Melody might have crossed, but that was what we needed to find out.

"So, whaddya need me to do?" she asked.

"I like that get-to-it spirit," I said, smiling. "I need you to rattle the gossip tree and see if Melody had any real enemies." I shook my head. "I just came back from the crime scene, and I have a couple of theories. First of all, I think it was a white or silver pickup. There was a sapling that had paint on it near the tire tracks. Also, the grass was tall, but undisturbed. I think a car, having lower ground clearance than a truck, would've disturbed the grass. So that's something, at least."

"Wow, Emma, that's some pretty good information for having just taken a look at the crime scene," Suzy replied. "I bet Tucker didn't catch any of that."

"You're right and he still thinks it was just a random accident," I said.

"Okay, Emma, of course I'll help you," she said. "Like we always said, one for all…"

"And all for one!" I replied.

"Speaking of, what about our third musketeer? Billy? Does he know about…your ability?" she asked, cocking up an eyebrow.

"Don't be mad, but yes…I told him, but it was when he was asking some medical questions about what my injuries were about," I confessed.

"It's okay, I get it," she said. "And I'm not surprised. I know you two have a *special* bond." She smirked.

Suzy was always trying to make more of my friendship with Billy than was actually there.

"Whatever!" I rolled my eyes. "Back to the topic at hand," I said, changing the subject. "Can you keep your ears peeled for any local gossip about Melody for me? I'm going to see what else I can find out about the crime scene."

I said goodbye to Suzy and headed up to the farm to do my daily chores. If I was visited by Melody's specter again, at least I had some solid questions to ask her.

CHAPTER 6

I didn't see Melody as I went about my daily chores, so I thought a visit to Melody's house, just at the outskirts of town, might yield some new information.

I stopped by our shed first and picked up a couple of pairs of the rubber gloves that Grandpa used when he was working on sick animals and shoved them into the pocket of my jeans. One thing I'd learned from detective shows, I didn't want to leave fingerprints anyplace the police might look later. If Tucker ever did realize he was dealing with a murder, I didn't want to disturb any important evidence.

Melody's house matched her perfectly. It was a small place right at the far edge of town. It looked like it had originally been one of the outer cottages of a local farm. It was a wooden house, painted white.

Outside, she had several patches of flowers in wild combinations. It reminded me of the English garden section of one of the botanical gardens I had visited. There were shocks of purple, and pink, yellow, and red. There were short, bushy patches of greenery, and tall, flowering plants.

Along the gardens edging were large, smooth river rocks, some of which were painted with colorful designs.

The front yard held about half a dozen birdhouses, and two bird baths. If any place had ever screamed eccentric artist, it was this one.

I went around to the back of the house, and found the back door unlocked. That was lucky, because I hadn't been quite sure how I would get in if the place was locked up tight with no spare key in sight.

I crept inside and looked around the kitchen. Nothing in there seemed really amiss. It was fairly neat and clean, with a lone coffee cup sitting, upside down, on top of a dish towel on the counter, as if Melody had walked out that morning, leaving it to dry. It was still so surreal to me to think someone I had spoken with in the afternoon would be dead by the evening.

As I started into the living room, I saw the mail bin attached to the wall near the kitchen door. I reached into my pocket and put on a pair of the rubber gloves. I grabbed the small stack of letters from the basket, flipping through them.

The first letter was a bill from Hollow Natural Gas. The next was a letter from the historical society, asking if Melody was going to participate in the Flower Festival auction by creating a banner. The third letter was from a lawyer's office. "Gamble & Gamble, Attorneys at Law," the envelope read, with a return address in Branson.

The letter thanked Melody for having visited their offices to discuss a wrongful death suit in the case of her beloved Golden Retriever, Claude.

I wonder if he was named Claude after Claude Monet, I speculated.

The letter went on to discuss legal fees and mentioned the prospective defendant by name: Dr. Jerry Langston.

Dr. Langston was the local veterinarian. He had been to

the farm to treat one of Grandpa's cows for some respiratory problem. I knew, though, that he also treated smaller animals, including pets. It was clear that Melody held Dr. Langston responsible if she was looking into suing him for the dog's death. He had also, strangely enough, aggressively pursued me to buy the banner I bought at the Flower Festival auction.

I tucked the letters back in the bin and headed into the living room. I was surprised to find it wasn't as neat as the kitchen, and in fact, it looked as though it had been ransacked. Along one wall was a small writing desk which had several drawers left hanging open. Another drawer was lying on its side on the floor. The accompanying desk chair had also been overturned.

There was no television in the living room, but on the wall opposite the desk was a large bookcase. It held several oversized pictorial books on artists, including Claude Monet, Whistler, and other masters. Some shelves also held large wicker baskets, each of which had been pulled out, and a couple of which had been overturned onto the floor.

In front of the small sofa was an oversized ottoman. A large, wooden serving tray on top of it turned it into a makeshift coffee table. On top of the tray was a small box that matched some of the ones on the higher shelves of the bookcase.

With my gloves on, I opened the box carefully. Inside there were dozens upon dozens of what looked like family photos. Some of them seemed to go back decades, while others were more recent, though I wouldn't say any of them looked new. Each photo contained Melody, and there was another figure cut out of most of them. A couple contained a younger woman, perhaps my age or a couple of years older, and a little girl.

As I dug around into the bottom of the box, my fingers

felt the smooth edge of a photo that had been cut into an oval. I carefully dumped the photos out onto the tray and was stunned to find dozens of pieces that had been cut from the photos, each of which depicted the same face – that of Melody's sister Cadence.

Melody and Cadence were what was sometimes referred to as Irish twins. They were less than a year apart in age and had been close most of their lives. Cadence was the caretaker at the local cemetery, and she also lived on the grounds there. I had to wonder what rift had occurred between them that had been so bad that Melody was literally trying to cut Cadence out of her life.

I walked through her bedroom, which was painted a pale blue, and had sparse furniture. The bed was made, and there was a large wardrobe across from the foot of the bed. I wasn't surprised as many old farm houses and cottages, my grandparents' place included, didn't have built-in closets. The doors of the wardrobe were open, but there were few contents save a few brightly colored, flowy tops on hangers and a few drawers, which had been pulled open.

Back in the hallway, beyond the bathroom was a glass-paned door that led out to a sunroom. The room was an obvious addition off the back side of the house. Opening the door with my gloved hand, I stepped through it, and into Melody's painting studio.

My first impression was that the space was at once cluttered and neat. I had known plenty of artists in New York, especially in the graphic design business. They were all a little quirky, but they typically kept their workspaces in some sort of special, chaotic order. Melody's studio was no exception.

There was a large drafting table in the corner. It was positioned so that the perfect amount of soft light hit the board, illuminating the paper or canvas with pure daylight that was perfect for sketching or painting. To the side of the drafting table was a small, three-tiered rolling cart full of pencils, markers, and paintbrushes on the top tier, with bottles of paints on the shelves below.

I sat on the stool and ran my hand across the paint-marred surface of the drafting table. I thought about all the happy hours Melody must've spent at that table creating her art.

I looked up from the drafting board to the cabinets across the room, and realized that they, like the living room, had been ransacked. The cabinet doors stood open, rolls of paper, canvases, and bins were strewn across the far side of the sun room.

What could they have been looking for?

Melody was clearly not impoverished, judging by her small but comfortable home. At the same time, she didn't appear to have much worth stealing, either. My grandparents lived a simple life on the farm that didn't come close to betraying the amount of money that they had stashed away. They could probably have afforded to buy any apartment in the city that they wanted, but instead, they lived frugally, enjoying the farm life. Melody, too, could have wealth that wasn't immediately obvious. Like my grandparents, though, if she did have money, it didn't appear to be in the house anywhere.

Whatever it was they were looking for, why would they be looking for it in Melody's studio?

Given the shelves and cabinets that had been rifled through, I couldn't help but wonder not only what the intruder had been after, but also whether or not they had found it.

As I let myself out through the kitchen door of Melody's home, I glanced around. Her refrigerator caught my eye. I stepped toward it, examining the items tacked to the front of it with small magnets. A couple of snapshots were attached to the freezer portion at the top. One was of a slim woman with dirty blonde hair that fell in waves to her shoulders. Her broad face was smiling widely at a little girl of about four years old. The child was clutching a flower in her chubby hand and appeared to be giving it to the woman who, judging by their similar appearance, must be her mother.

The woman in the photo looked like Melody with her slender nose, broad face, and wavy hair, though Melody's had long since gone gray. I remembered that she had a daughter named Kayla, but I didn't know her. The next snapshot was more recent. Melody was on the far left of the photo, the woman from the other photo, which I could see now had to be Kayla, in the middle, and a young girl of about eight, who must be Melody's granddaughter.

On the bottom section of the refrigerator door there were several children's drawings held by magnets as well. One showed a little blonde girl and a lady with gray hair, drawn as stick figures, holding hands and smiling. The older figure had the word *grandma* written beside it with an arrow pointing to the figure. The smaller figure had the word *me* scrawled beside it, followed by what looked like an errant vertical crayon mark, and had a similar arrow pointing to the child.

I left Melody's and texted Suzy to see if she could meet me to chat. She said that Brian was there and he had just put some burgers on the grill but invited me to come over and have dinner.

CHAPTER 7

When I arrived, Suzy met me at the door.

"Hi," she said, opening it and ushering me in.

"Thanks for having me," I replied. "Is Brian…" I started to ask his whereabouts as I looked around.

"He's out back, manning the grill," she replied. "We've got a minute."

"Oh, great. So first off, nothing about what I told you in front of Brian, okay? I mean, I know he's your fiancé, and I trust him, of course, but…I don't know. I feel weird enough that you and Billy know." I looked down at my feet. I still felt a little embarrassed and the whole idea of seeing spirits, or as far as Suzy knew just having psychic intuition, still felt a little crazy to me.

"Oh, honey!" Suzy said, hugging my neck, "I would never share something you asked me not to. Even with Brian! One for all," she started our best friend saying and before I could finish, there was a knock on the front door just behind us.

"Ah, that timing could not have been better!" Suzy chuckled. She kept her eyes locked on me as she opened the front door. "Hi, Billy," she said, never looking up at him.

"Uh, hi, Suzy," he replied, obviously noticing her lack of eye contact. "I guess you knew it was me, huh?"

Billy stepped inside, filling the small foyer with his height and broad shoulders. His dark hair was shiny as if he had just washed it. It was ridiculous. How did the kid I spent every day of my childhood with, the one who I had personally seen laugh so hard that chocolate milk shot out his nose not once, but twice – how did that goofy kid grow up to look like that?

"Emma." He looked down at me, smiling as he walked toward the kitchen, an eight pack of pops in one hand. "I'm starved! Let's go out back," he said, clapping his palm on my shoulder.

I greeted Brian, thanking him for making us dinner. We all sat down around the outdoor dining set. The big open yard had a flower garden at the back that was blooming with a riot of color. A few large trees scattered around the perimeter, just inside the tall wooden fence, made the space feel cozy and comfortable.

"These burgers are great, Brian," Billy said, taking a big bite. I agreed and after we finished eating, Suzy and I cleaned up. It gave me a chance to tell her about my adventures that afternoon.

"So, you broke into her house?" Suzy exclaimed as we rinsed the dishes at her kitchen sink.

"Shh! No, of course not!" I replied. "The door was open. I just…sort of…let myself in."

"Emma! You're going to get arrested!" She shook her head and heaved a heavy sigh. "But, as long as you're taking this whole thing seriously enough to engage in criminal *be-hav-iorrr…*," she exaggerated the last word, casting a side-eyed glance my way, "what did you find out?"

"Well, for a start, I wasn't the first one to go in there. The place was ransacked. Not everywhere, and not every room. Someone went through every cabinet, shelf, and drawer in her living room, and emptied all the cabinets in her studio, too. Other things seemed to be left alone, though – like her bedroom, and kitchen – they were neat as a pin." I shrugged.

"Wow! What do you think they were looking for?" Suzy asked.

"I'm not sure…and whatever it was, I'm not sure they found it. There was something else, too," I said, poking my head around Suzy to look outside.

Through the glass doors to the deck, I could see Billy and Brian were still sitting at the table, talking and laughing.

"There was a letter from a lawyer in her mail basket. It looks like Melody was suing Dr. Langston. Something about wrongful death for her Golden Retriever, Claude," I said.

"Oh, yes! I had forgotten all about him! She loved that dog. She took him everywhere. He was really sweet but seemed to be very old. She was even more of a misery than usual after he passed away," Suzy said, shaking her head.

I thought of sweet little Halee, and how devastated Billy would be if anything happened to her.

"The other weird thing," I continued, glancing toward the glass doors again, "was the photos of her and her sister, Cadence. There was a box with tons of pictures of the two of them, and in every single one, Cadence's face had been cut from the photo. It was…well, the only word to describe it is creepy," I said.

Suzy shuddered. "Creepy is right! I can't imagine the level of hate you would need to cut your own sister out of a bunch of photos." Suzy walked to the refrigerator and grabbed a bowl of fruit salad topped with whipped cream. "Come on, we'd better get back before those boys come looking for us. Grab those bowls and spoons for me?" She nodded toward a stack on the counter, and I complied.

"Dessert!" Suzy said triumphantly, holding the glass bowl up to show off the pretty, striped layers of fruit before setting it on the table outside.

"Very nice, hon!" Brian said, putting his hand on her back and giving it a loving rub up and down as Suzy sat.

"Thank you!" she replied sweetly, planting a quick kiss on his lips as she grabbed the serving spoon. They really were a great couple. "Okay, pass me your bowl," she said, serving Brian first, then scooping out a large helping for Billy. "Bowl, Emma." She motioned toward me with the serving spoon, keeping it hovering over the bowl so that the juices from the berries didn't spill all over.

"I don't think so, thanks," I replied.

"Emma! It's just fruit! Bowl!" She gave me a look, and I handed her my bowl obediently.

I looked at Billy, and he looked back at me. We both mouthed the word at the same time. *Bossy!*

"I see you two, you know. You're not cute," Suzy said playfully, rolling her eyes as she served herself.

"I don't know, Suz," Billy said, smiling broadly. "I think we're pretty adorable." He turned and winked at me before tucking back into the bowl of sweet fruit for another bite. We all laughed.

"So..." Suzy said, looking at me to signal she was shifting the conversation. "How about that business with Melody Campbell?" She shook her head. "What an awful way to go."

"Yeah, it's awful," Brian said. "I can't believe someone would have an accident like that and just keep going without...I don't know, trying to help or something!"

"Well, that's the part I'm not so sure about," Billy chimed in. "I'm not sure it was an accident. The whole thing just didn't add up for me."

"Right! You were called out right when it happened, huh?"

Brian replied. "So you think someone – would someone have hit her on purpose?"

"Well, I had heard," Suzy chimed in, "that she had some enemies. I mean, she was really talented, and I never had problems with her, but the woman was a bit...oh, I can't speak ill of the dead! Let's just say she was different."

"You know, it was really strange...Dr. Langston came up to me after the banner auction and tried to get me to sell him the banner I bought for Grandma. It was one of Melody's," I said.

"Which is weird, right? Because I heard she blamed him for Claude's death," Suzy added. "You know, her dog?"

"Yeah, he told me about that," Billy said. "I mean, we run into each other sometimes. He has come by the clinic to borrow supplies a couple of times when he ran out of something simple like packing gauze."

"Really? What did he say?" I asked.

"Well, she was furious when Claude passed away," Billy said. "But the poor thing was fifteen years old. He couldn't live forever." He shook his head. "I mean, I love Halee – I get it, but it wasn't Jerry's fault."

"She had some family, right?" I asked, knowing the answer but hoping either Brian or Billy would know more.

"She has a daughter, Kayla, and a granddaughter," Billy said.

"And then there's the sister." Brian rolled his eyes. "If you thought Melody was a little...well, odd – you should try talking to Cadence!"

"Oh, yeah? What's her story?" I asked.

"She's the groundskeeper over at the cemetery. You know we have a family plot over there. All the Baileys going back eight generations are buried in that cemetery, and my mom and aunts go over there every holiday – you know, Easter, Memorial Day, and so forth, to put flowers and flags on the gravestones of all the family members and make sure they're all kept up," Brian said.

"All the Baileys are into family history," Suzy added proudly. "They can trace their family back to the first Baileys to come to America just before the revolutionary war." She smiled.

"That's right," Brian said, rubbing her shoulder lovingly. "Anyway, Cadence lives in the caretaker shack over on the cemetery grounds."

"Yeah, she's odd. In fact, I mean, I hate to even say it..." Billy hesitated. "But I've seen her in town a few times when I've had to go into the clinic at night or on the weekends, and...well, she was going through the trash in the back of the businesses." He shook his head. "Lena told me once she saw her going through the clothing donation bins in the back of the church, too."

"That's awful!" I said. "If she was so bad off, why wouldn't Melody help her?"

"Don't get me wrong – I don't think she's going hungry or anything, but I've seen her pull a piece of furniture out of a dumpster, stuff like that," Billy quickly added.

I had often seen people curb diving in the city for discarded furniture or old store stock. I'd never heard of it in a town as small as Hillbilly Hollow, though.

We chatted a little longer before both Billy and I got up to leave. I thanked Suzy and Brian for dinner and told Suzy I'd call her the next day. Billy walked me outside to my car.

"Goodnight." I waved, opening the door to the truck.

"Not so fast there, Emma," Billy's voice was deep and stern – his doctor voice – as he took a few steps and was standing directly in front of me in a moment. Darn him and that six-foot-two stride of his.

"Hmm?" I made the questioning sound innocently. He met my feigned ignorance with a raised eyebrow.

"Come on, what's up?" he asked. "Please tell me you're not getting mixed up in this business with Melody Campbell."

"No, I was just…I just…" I stammered, not wanting to lie. *Sugar! Why does he always see right through me?* "I just have a naturally curious nature." I smiled, proud of the not-quite-lie.

Billy rolled his eyes. "I know that trying to get something through that hard head of yours is about as difficult as getting an old hound dog to back off a treed coon," he said, "but can you at least promise me you'll be careful? I don't want you gettin' hurt, Emma. I've kinda gotten used to you being back in town." He idly touched a curl that had fallen forward and lay on top of my shoulder with the tips of his fingers. "If you cross the wrong person, and they hurt you… well, I did take the Hippocratic oath, after all. Ya know, *first do no harm?* So, it wouldn't really do for me to have to put the beat down on somebody for hurtin' my friend." He smiled.

"I can take care of myself, you know." I raised an eyebrow defensively and crossed my arms.

"So says the woman who I've treated for a bruised rib from a goat kick, and a tetanus shot for a chicken-inflicted laceration." He chuckled.

"Okay, okay, point taken," I said, heaving a sigh. "I promise I'll be careful, and if I need you?"

"You don't have to ask – just say the word," he said. "One for all…"

"And all for one!" I replied.

CHAPTER 8

The next day, I helped Grandpa do some fence mending around the livestock pasture. Mr. Piper was the man whose farm backed up to ours on the far side of the grazing pasture. Mr. Piper had a particularly friendly young bull that kept slipping into our pasture to get friendly with Grandpa's cows and Grandpa was determined to put a stop to it.

I asked Grandpa how well he knew Melody and Cadence Campbell, as we worked.

"As well as anybody, I suppose," he said. He was a man of few words, my Grandpa.

"Do you know if there was some sort of disagreement between them?" I asked cautiously. "I heard some talk in town that they didn't get on."

"Oh, now you'd have to ask your Grandma if it's gossip you're looking for," he said. "That quilting circle of hers does such a good job of keeping her in the know, she's likely to know about things that didn't even happen!" He gave a rare chuckle, proud of himself for having made a joke.

"That was a good one, Grandpa!" I smiled at him.

"As far as Cadence and Melody, though, I'm not sure. Neither of them ever married, that much I know," he said.

"Hmpf," I replied. I decided I would ask Grandma about the issues between the sisters. She was in the heart of Hillbilly Hollow gossip central after all – the quilting circle.

After we finished the fence mending, I went back to the house to talk to Grandma.

Snowball had followed me and Grandpa as we did our chores around the farm that morning, and when I headed back, she hopped up from the shady spot in which she was lying and followed me down the worn path in the grass back to the house.

It was lunchtime, and the satellite service guy should have been arriving any minute. I made myself a tuna sandwich, tossing Snowball a stalk of celery to munch on, and before too long there was a knock at the front door.

When I answered the door, a man who I didn't know but who looked familiar as someone from town was standing on the other side of it. I looked around him and saw that his truck had a magnet on the side that read: *A-1 Electronic Installation (TV 2 You Contract Installer)*.

He came in and told me a couple things he said I would need to know about the internet service and television package. He put a few things inside the house, then went back out to put the satellite dish on the roof. I walked out with him and made it a point to tell him to put the dish on the far side of the roof. Grandma still had her occasional funny spells, as Grandpa called them, wherein she would climb up onto the roof, and sing to the chickens in the middle of the night. I didn't want her having an episode, finding an unfamiliar item on the roof in the form of a satellite dish, and freaking out, possibly hurting herself.

After the installation was complete, I grabbed my laptop and the technician showed me how everything was set up and how to connect to the Wi-Fi. I was thrilled to pull up a webpage and find it load almost right away, instead of the interminable wait using my hotspot. If I was going to do a bit of freelance graphic design work so I could keep earning some money, reliable internet would be crucial.

The technician also showed Grandma how to use the new cable box I had gotten for her and Grandpa. They were perfectly content watching the same four channels day in and day out, but I knew they would enjoy the old movies channel, and the channel that showed all the wholesome shows they enjoyed.

After the technician was gone, I joined Grandma on the sofa to ask about Melody and Cadence.

"Melody had a daughter, right? Kayla?" I asked after Grandma confirmed what Grandpa had said earlier – that the two women had definitely had some sort of rift between them.

"She did, and quite the scandal that was back in their day," Grandma confirmed. "She and Cadence, you see, well they were both after the same man. They had always been close, the sisters. They used to load up in the summertime and go selling Melody's artwork at festivals and craft fairs around the country. To hear Cadence tell it, they both fell for some potter from down in Alabama that was on the same festival circuit. So, Cadence decides she's gonna follow this fella around the country, then she finds out that Melody is pregnant with his baby. They came home, and Cadence moved out the next day, got the job over at the cemetery and she's been there ever since."

"Wow, that's kinda crazy," I said. "So, they stopped talking, all because of a man?" I asked.

"No, Cadence got over it in time," Grandma replied. "She and Melody were just different. Melody was a little quirky, to be sure. She could be so sarcastic, it was enough to drive you bonkers. Cadence is a little different, though. Cadence just wants so badly to get off that cemetery property and make a nice life for herself."

Grandma continued, "The problem is, Cadence isn't the brightest crayon in the box. She was always one to have some crazy scheme or idea, but never had any idea how to make it work – even if the idea was good. She wanted something better but had no idea how to get it."

"Wow, that's kind of sad," I said. "It's a shame they weren't closer." In my mind, I was thinking about the photos I saw in Melody's house. There was definitely something a bit deeper there between Cadence and Melody – I just wasn't sure what.

* * *

I TALKED with Grandma a little while longer and decided to go down to town to enjoy some of the Flower Festival activities. There was a street party that evening in the park and along Main Street. Local restaurants and food trucks set up to sell food, and the street was blocked off as a makeshift dance floor with a band playing at the park entrance. I knew Grandma and Grandpa would go, lawn chairs in tow, no doubt. I had texted Suzy earlier and agreed to meet her and Brian there.

I took a nice soak in the bathtub to get ready to go down to the festival and washed my hair. The bathtub was in the laundry room – the only room in the house, save the kitchen, that had plumbing. Since I'd been home, Snowball and I had become virtually inseparable. She liked to hang out in the laundry room while I bathed or washed my clothes, so I made her a little bed from an old storage bin and a groom's blanket, which I made a cushion from by stuffing it with batting. As soon as I set it up, she hopped right in, understanding it was just for her.

After my bath, I went upstairs to choose something to wear. I had really made the old attic pretty cozy. The bed Grandpa constructed for the twin-sized mattress I bought made it really comfortable. The clothing rack I was using as a makeshift closet held all my clothes and shoes nicely, and I had even found a little writing desk at Secondhand Rose, the thrift store in town, which doubled as both a workspace for my laptop, and a great place to sit and apply my makeup. The farm was definitely becoming home again.

I flipped through some of the options I had that would be appropriate for the evening. I had brought a handful of sundresses with me and ordered a few more since I'd been there. Hillbilly Hollow didn't have quite the shopping options that New York had, but thanks to the internet, most of my favorite brands were as close as our mailbox.

I found the bright green sundress with the floral motif that was one of my favorites and hung it up on the edge of the clothing rack, facing outward. As I looked at the dress, I realized it reminded me of Melody. The green background with the abstract flower pattern reminded me of the garden at her house, and for some reason, I thought she, in particular, would like this dress with its artistic print.

My hair had gotten long since I'd been home. The weather was supposed to be nice – not too hot – so I styled my hair in loose curls down my back. I put on a little makeup and donned the sundress and a pair of sandals with a low heel. I twirled around in front of the dorm mirror I had propped up next to the clothing rack and checked myself out. I looked pretty good, if I said so myself. I popped my keys, phone, ID and some cash into a little wristlet bag and headed out.

When I got to town, I parked up by the clinic and walked

down to the park. I paid the cover charge to enter the festival, all ten dollars of which went to the Hillbilly Hollow Historical Society, of which I was a member.

The Flower Festival committee had done a great job on the event. There were white lights strewn back and forth across Main Street, and the band that was playing was actually pretty good. I didn't see Suzy and Brian, so I stood at the edge of the bandstand, listening for a few minutes.

"Hello, Emma," a voice said from behind me. I turned around to find Tucker standing behind me. "Enjoying the festival?"

I was taken aback. He was out of uniform, wearing jeans and a polo shirt. The blue of his shirt made his blonde hair and beard stand out even more, and really set off his blue eyes. He really was a handsome man. It was a shame his brains didn't match his brawn.

"I am, thanks. Looks like you are too – off duty tonight?" I asked.

"Yeah, I decided to let the boys handle it tonight." He nodded. "I haven't taken a day off in a while."

"Well, it's a great night for it, and the Flower Festival society did a great job putting it together," I said.

As we stood and chatted, Tucker's eyes suddenly got as big as saucers. "Oh, no," he muttered under his breath.

"What's wrong?" I asked.

"Patrice Patterson, twelve o'clock. Darn it! I don't think I can hide from her," he said, his brow furrowing.

"Why would you…" I started to ask.

Patrice was interrupting us before I could finish my thought. "There you are, *Tucker*," she said, cooing his name. "I've been looking for you all evening."

"Hello, Ms. Patterson," he said, slipping into professional mode.

"Patrice! I've told you to call me Patrice," she said raising an eyebrow. "I was hoping I could pry a dance out of you."

"Oh, I-I'm sorry, *Patrice*," he said her name carefully and it did not appear to roll easily off his tongue. Although I was disappointed at the interruption – I had wanted to get some information out of Tucker regarding Melody's death – I was amused watching the middle-aged, platinum blonde try to pick up the local sheriff.

"Yeah, so sorry, but I was just about to dance with Emma here. Come on, Emma," he said, grabbing my hand and leading me out into the middle of the street.

What was happening? I wasn't sure how I ended up in the middle of the street, dancing with the sheriff, but that was exactly where I found myself. A slightly upbeat ballad was playing, and he slipped one hand around my waist, taking my hand in his other one. I was surprised to find him a good dancer.

"Sheriff Tucker!" I laughed. "You have some serious dance moves!"

He spun me around once and pulled me back in a half-dip.

"Thanks, Emma. You shouldn't discount us big guys as not being agile, you know. I played football in both high school and college." He smiled. "You have to have some pretty good moves there too, ya know."

As we finished our dance, I saw Suzy and Brian walking up. "Thanks for the dance, Emma. You really saved me." He smiled.

"Happy to help, Tucker, and it was fun!" I reached up and patted him gently on the shoulder.

There was no chemistry between Tucker and me by any stretch of the imagination, but I hadn't been on a date since before I'd had my accident in New York, and I couldn't lie.

Dancing and flirting a little were fun, even if it didn't mean a thing.

"Were you dancing with Tucker?" Suzy asked as soon as she walked up.

"I was." I laughed. "Patrice Patterson was trying to catch him in her snare, and he needed rescuing."

"Oh!" Suzy laughed too. "Yes, Patrice can be very enthusiastic when it comes to eligible men!" Patrice was attractive, but she was quite a bit older than Tucker, with very exaggerated hair and makeup and wore over-the-top outfits. She was a total cougar.

"I was just talking to Sherrie Selby on our way in," Suzy said, leaning in to whisper as Brian said hello to some guys passing by. "She said Jennie Weaver came back to work acting very smug. Said that Jennie even made a passing comment that Melody wouldn't be bothering her or anybody else anymore thanks to Dylan – Dylan Shepherd. That's her boyfriend. Can you believe that? It's a morbid thing to say, if you ask me."

"Wow!" I exclaimed. "So, do you think that…I mean, surely Jennie and Dylan wouldn't have murdered an old lady. Do you think?"

"I don't know, Emma. I mean, that's a pretty cold comment, but murder? I just don't know." Suzy shook her head.

"I don't mean to interrupt this meeting of the brain trust." Brian smirked. "But Emma, do you mind if I steal my beautiful fiancé away for a dance?"

"Not at all!" I smiled at Brian and patted him on the arm. He really was great, and I was so happy he and Suzy had found each other.

As I wandered around the grounds, perusing the delicious goods on display at each food truck, I saw Jennie Weaver with her boyfriend, and a few other rough-looking characters in their early twenties milling around at the end of the row of food trucks. They were passing something back and forth, careful to keep their backs to the crowd. *Beer,* I thought, *or worse, moonshine.*

Our little gang had done our fair share of carrying on and acting silly but it mostly ended when everyone went off to college. For this group, though, that was clearly not their path. They didn't have the luxury of college. Instead, they graduated from high school, if they were lucky, and found the first job they could. Some waited tables or tended bar at the Mexican restaurant out on the far end of the highway. Others fixed cars and took odd jobs. Some, the ones who were willing to work hard and keep regular hours, went to work at the dog food plant.

If you were from Happy Hills, working at the plant was a good job, and one you were likely to try your best to hold onto. That didn't make much difference, though, when the plant closed down. Hundreds of people from three counties were all out of work. It was a hard blow to the area, and even harder to the families who relied on the plant for most of their income. I wasn't surprised that some of the former plant workers were among those raising a little Cain in the park.

I walked over to where the row of food trucks and tents stood and got some lemonade and a funnel cake. I may not be in my twenties anymore, and couldn't eat junk food like I used to, but if indulging in a funnel cake meant I'd have to do a few extra chores the next day to work it off, it was definitely worth the efforts.

I sat at one of the picnic tables that had been set up in long rows near the food stalls. I made small talk with a few people I knew, and others I recognized from around town but didn't know well. A few people emptied out from the table at which I sat to wander around the carnival-like atmosphere, and I happily tucked into my funnel cake.

With fewer people around, the voices at the table behind me became more prominent. There was a voice I recognized as being familiar, but that I couldn't quite place – a man's voice – and he was speaking to a woman. Their exchange was clearly meant to be quiet, but with the thinned crowd, their whisper-yell of conversation became audible. I concentrated to hear what they were saying.

"Look, the way things have been, I just don't think we can afford..." the woman said before the man cut her off.

"Myrna, don't worry! I told you, it's taken care of!" the man replied.

"There could be an estate! What if the daughter..." again, the man cut her off.

"No, no, no! I told you! We're good! It's all covered. I've taken care of it," the man replied.

"If you would run your business properly we wouldn't have this problem! I mean, you can't spend your time driving around the county, doing this and that for people's animals, and take payment in chickens!" The woman's voice had turned from worried to annoyed.

Someone else walked up and interrupted the conversation. "Good evening," a strong, deep voice I recognized said. 'You folks havin' a good night?"

"Oh yeah, Will, real good. You?" The man said. I was right – it was Billy's voice I had heard.

"Great, thanks. Just got here. Myrna, you look lovely as ever." The woman giggled at the compliment.

"Hey, I'm going to join some friends. Good seeing you though, Jerry. Myrna."

So, it was Jerry and Myrna Langston I had overheard after all.

I wonder what he was talking about when he said he had taken care of everything?

I heard the steps behind me and turned around to find Billy standing over me.

"Hi." I smiled up at him, but he wasn't smiling.

"Where's Tucker?" he said, still serious.

"Um… I have no idea. Why? Everything okay?" I replied, trying to read the reason behind his expression.

"Well, it's none of my business, but it seems pretty rude for him to just leave you sitting here by yourself," he huffed.

"What is your problem? Here, sit." I patted the bench next to me. "Help me eat this funnel cake."

"I wouldn't want to horn in, Emma," he said, looking around, his arms crossed.

"Billy Stone, sit your butt down before I get up and kick it!" I said, channeling some voice from our middle school years.

He followed the direction.

"Now," I said, "what in the world is your problem?"

"I don't have a problem. I just think it's pretty crappy for a guy to walk off and leave his date."

"Okay, look, I've had a kind of long day and you are making no sense right now. Plain English, please?" I replied, growing exasperated.

"I heard you were here with Tucker. You two are some sort of an item now?" His tone was still short.

I laughed out loud. "Are you nuts? No way!"

"You're not here with him?" he asked the question as if trying to catch me in a lie.

"As if!" I rolled my eyes. "No, you big doofus! I am not here with Tucker."

"Oh," he said, looking off into the distance. "I heard you were here together. Somebody said they saw you dancing earlier, and…" He trailed off.

"I was dancing with him. Patrice Patterson was stalking him, so he asked me to dance to get away from her." I laughed. "Dude, you weren't...you're not jealous, are you? Come on! You've got nothing to worry about! If I were dating someone, you'd be the first person to know." I punched him in the shoulder. "Idiot," I said, shaking my head.

"Oh," he said, smirking a little. "That's good then. I shouldn't hear about something like that secondhand." He leaned over and pulled a piece off my funnel cake and dropped it into his mouth.

"Besides, it's not like there are exactly a zillion eligible bachelors in Hillbilly Hollow," I said, shrugging.

"Right," Billy said, grabbing my lemonade and downing a big gulp.

"Hey," I leaned in and kept my voice down. "Did you hear what Dr. Langston and his wife were talking about?"

"No, I just stopped to say hi. Why?" Billy replied.

"I just...I don't know. I caught a snippet of their conversation and it sounded...I don't know." I couldn't get out of my head what Dr. Langston had said. How he had taken care of everything.

Billy was looking around, when something out on the street caught his eye. "No way!" he said, craning his neck as a smile crept across his face. "You gotta see this!" he said, grabbing my hand and pulling me to my feet.

He dragged me across the park to the street, where the band had shifted gears and was playing an old big band song. There, amongst the old couples who were up and dancing, in the middle of it all, were my Grandma and Grandpa. Grandma looked beautiful. Her face shone up at Grandpa who was looking at her with his eyes filled with love. They moved so gracefully. I felt a drop of water breach my eyelashes, and quickly lifted a finger to wipe it away.

"Aw, Emma! Are you crying?" Billy said, smiling empathetically.

"No! You're crying! Shut up!" We both laughed.

"Come on." He tugged on my hand, and pulled me to the street to dance alongside them. Grandma looked over and smiled, and Grandpa gave Billy a little wink. We mimicked their posture, Billy holding one hand up for me to take, and putting the other around my back as I put my hand on his shoulder.

"They've known each other since grade school, ya know," Billy whispered. "They're pretty great, huh?"

I looked over to my grandparents and nodded in agreement. *They are pretty great. And I'm pretty lucky,* I thought.

WE FOUND Suzy and Brian and hung out the rest of the evening. Several other people from school stopped by and chatted throughout the night. Fair food was my weakness, and I ate so many funnel cakes, corn dogs, and churros that I was afraid I might puke.

Grandma and Grandpa were long-since in bed by the time I got home. I was content from a fun evening as I parked the farm truck.

But when I walked across the front porch, something seemed amiss. I took a step back and looked around. Melody's banner – the one I had bought for Grandma at the Flower Festival auction…it was gone!

CHAPTER 9

The next day, I asked Grandma at breakfast if she had taken down the Flower Festival banner.

The thing wasn't exactly my cup of tea. It was a slightly impressionist design, with brightly colored flowers along the bottom, and a background of medium and dark green tones. Off to the left of the picture was a cylindrical looking shape of dark grays and browns, and just beyond it was a black shape that looked almost like a human figure. It was classic Melody, with the impressionist style and bold colors. There was something sort of familiar about the scene. It reminded me of those pictures where you have to squint slightly to see beyond the random shapes for the picture to come into focus.

Grandma was cooking bacon when I walked into the kitchen. It smelled Heavenly. Clearly, eating fair food like a thirteen-year-old boy the night before had done nothing to stave off my hunger the next morning.

"Good morning, Grandma," I said.

"Emma, dear! Good morning!" She smiled and stuck her cheek out for a kiss, which I promptly planted there.

I grabbed a plate with a blue cornflower pattern around the outside edge and sat down at the small, round kitchen table. Grandma deposited three slices of bacon, some toast and a sunny-side-up egg on my plate.

"Thanks, Grandma!"

I sometimes felt a bit selfish for letting her serve me breakfast, but the few times I had tried to make it for myself, she spent the whole day in a huff. She was just about the sweetest woman in the world and feeling like she was taking care of whoever was in the house seemed to give her utter joy.

She grabbed a cup of strong, black coffee, and sat down beside me.

"When I came in last night, I noticed the banner was missing. Did you take it down?" I asked.

"The one you got me from the festival? Oh, no! I didn't touch it," she said. "I don't think your Grandpa has either." She held her coffee cup in one hand, and turned it round and round in the other, worriedly. "I can't imagine someone coming all the way up here just to take it, can you?"

I had to admit, it didn't seem likely, but it was clearly not where it had been before.

I finished my breakfast and helped Grandma in the vegetable garden for a bit. Snowball found a little patch of sunshine and lounged beside us as we worked. This was her favorite chore on the farm. She knew if there were vegetables that were too riddled with insects, or that had grown into weird, stunted shapes, she would get them as a treat.

After a morning in the garden, we spent the better part of the afternoon pickling cucumbers and okra. It was a gorgeous day outside, so I decided to take a walk down to Ford's Cross, the small lake near our house. Snowball followed behind me as we trotted down the twisty trail toward the lake. We had gotten just a short distance into the woods, not far from where our backyard ended, when a shock of color across a small bush near the edge of the trail caught my attention.

As I got closer, I could see it was a piece of fabric. Strange, considering how only true locals typically went to Ford's Cross, and people who grew up in the area, for the most part, had enough respect for its natural beauty not to litter. I walked closer to examine the fabric, thinking I could take it back to the farmhouse to be thrown away. As I leaned forward to untangle it from the shrub, I drew in a stunned breath. It was the banner from our porch!

As I untangled the banner, I could see that a large swath of it was missing, and judging by the charred marks on the fabric, appeared to have been burned away. The piece that was left was the bottom, right-hand corner. The remaining piece of the banner had a green background and the name *M. Campbell* scrawled in white paint. I carefully folded the piece of fabric and tucked it into the pocket of my pants, and continued my walk.

Making my way down to Ford's Cross, I thought about the other houses and farms in the area, wondering who, among their residence, would do something as hateful and unnecessary as to first steal, then destroy, the banner my Grandma loved so much. The banner had not been cheap, either. I had just beat out Lisa Teller-Parks for it, and had to pay a pretty penny to get it. Suddenly, I remembered my conversation at the auction.

Jerry Langston!

He had wanted the banner badly, and tried to bully me into selling it to him just after I'd purchased it.

Dr. Langston and his wife Myrna had a small horse farm back behind what used to be the Stone farm, where Billy had grown up. It wasn't exactly adjacent to our property, but it wasn't that far either, and the trail down to Ford's Cross would make it easy for Dr. Langston to get from his place to ours unnoticed.

Why in the world would he try so hard to get the banner, only to destroy it? None of it made sense to me.

I wandered around down near the water for a while, trying to clear my head, but couldn't relax. I decided to go back up to the house. It seemed that Melody's poor dog, Claude, had probably died of old age. Still, that didn't stop her heart from breaking over it, or stop her from blaming Dr. Langston.

Would a lawsuit that he was likely to win anyway, be enough to kill over?

I had to wonder. He had said he had *taken care* of the Melody problem when we were at the festival the other night, though. Thanks to the new internet connection that Grandpa had finally conceded to letting me add, I could dig around online and see if I could learn any more about Dr. Langston or any other lawsuits Melody had up her sleeve.

* * *

I ENTERED MY ATTIC ROOM, and carefully removed the folded remnant of the banner from my pocket, placing it on the shelf atop my makeshift closet. For a moment, I wished that my – gift? ability? – whatever it was, allowed me to conjure up the spirits who contacted me when I needed them. I had questions, and Melody might actually be of some use, but there was no way to know if, or when, I might see her again.

At my little, makeshift desk, I started searching online for records in the county civil courts. I searched using a couple of variants of Melody's name, but to no avail. Searches under Dr. Langston's name didn't pull up anything either. I decided to take a different route, and pull up any hits for area news stories that mentioned either of them. One of those annoying pop-up ads appeared on-screen, and I was about to close it until I realized what it was advertising.

The ad was for a popular website that had started as a news and information forum, but had evolved over time to be a source of gossip and speculation, especially in small towns. I saw the locales listed on the ad.

Springfield, Branson...Hillbilly Hollow.

Who knew that our little town would have its own, dedicate sub-forum? I clicked on it immediately.

The site required me to create a login, and I decided on *ArtyGirl06.* The postings were on a wide variety of topics. There were plenty of ads for people buying and selling various goods. There were so many ads looking for romance, I found it a bit disturbing. There were only about five-thousand people in town, after all.

Who might they be looking for, that they don't already know? I wondered.

Finally, something of interest to me caught my eye. The topic heading read, *Who Robbed Chapmans?*

The day before Melody was killed, Chapman's store had been robbed at gunpoint. Tucker and his motley crew seemed sure that it was some passerby who had happened through town with the rest of the Flower Festival traffic. I wasn't so sure. I opened the link for the robbery topic on the forum, and went through the posts and replies.

One person, who called themselves *HollowGal59* said that she thought it was someone from Keener, a little town between Hillbilly Hollow and Springfield. Her reasoning was that Old Fort Days and the Flower Festival drew such huge crowds, and the Keener Homecoming Festival had dropped in attendance over recent years. I wasn't sure that small-town festival sabotage was a likely motive for robbery, so I moved on.

Another poster thought it might have been someone from

the trailer park at the edge of town. According to *Regular_Joe*, the residents of the park had fallen on particularly hard times since the dog food plant a couple of towns over had closed the year before, putting many of them out of work. That seemed like the most reasonable idea I had read. Happy Hills was just on the outskirts of town, and there were definitely a few unsavory characters in the area.

A reply to Regular_Joe's post caught my attention. "Not everybody got a good job, JOE BOYLE," wrote *JennieJennie1995*, "there's good people living up in Happy Hills. Not everybody's a criminal just cause they're poor, ya know!" From the tone of the post, I knew it had to be Jennie Weaver. I wondered if her boyfriend, Dylan, was living in Happy Hills. He was definitely a rough sort of guy. I didn't like to think anyone was capable of murder, but Jennie had made some snide comments about Melody's death, and Melody had tried to get Jennie fired. It felt to me like that could've been a motive for Dylan to want to take revenge on Melody.

I was starting to detect a familiar smell wafting up through the floorboards of my attic room, and went down to the kitchen to investigate. Grandpa was sitting on the sofa watching a game show.

"Hi, Grandpa," I said, plopping down next to him. "Whitewater rafting."

"What's that, then?" he asked.

"The puzzle – the answer is whitewater rafting." I smiled proudly just as the contestant on TV blurted out the answer.

"I'll be darned," Grandpa replied, patting my knee. "You are a pretty smart cookie, aren't ya?"

I decided to ask him how to broach the subject of the stolen banner with Grandma. "Can I ask you something? I need to talk to Grandma, and I'm not sure what to say," I said to him sheepishly.

"Oh? Everything alright, Emma?" He uncharacteristically

turned his attention away from the television, and gave it all to me. We hadn't always been as close as we might have been, but when he looked at me, when he looked into my eyes, it was an older version of my own eyes I saw staring back at me. My parents had been gone for such a long time that I was rarely around anyone who shared my features. Looking into my Grandpa and Grandma's faces gave me that unique sense of comfort.

"Yes, it's just that…well, someone stole the banner. The one I bought at the Flower Festival auction? Someone took it from the front porch. I noticed it the other night, and Grandma said she hadn't taken it down, and you hadn't either."

"Oh." He looked serious, and raked a callused thumb and finger across the five-o'clock shadow of his chin. "Is that right?"

"Yes, and when I was out for a walk this afternoon…well, I found what was left of it on the trail to Ford's Cross. It had been burned, all except for one small corner. Isn't it strange?"

"Strange indeed," Grandpa replied, looking off as if he were turning something over in his mind. "People don't typically come up here by accident, ya know. Dorothy loved that banner. Can't imagine who would want to hurt her by destroying it."

"Well, it was so strange…when I bought it at the auction, a couple of people bid on it, but Lisa Teller-Parks wanted it pretty bad, and seemed angry when I won it. Then Dr. Langston came up to me after the auction and tried to get me to sell it to him. He was pretty adamant that he get it, but I wouldn't give it up."

"Langston? Oh, no!" Grandpa chuckled. "Jerry wouldn't hurt a fly. Now Myrna, on the other hand…I wouldn't put stealing something so someone else couldn't have it past her a bit. She's a spiteful old woman, that Myrna," Grandpa said.

He looked away, into the distance, then turned back to me. "Let's keep this between us, Emma. I don't want your Grandma to know someone would steal something she loved just so they could destroy it. Better for her to think they stole it because they wanted it for themselves."

"That's a good idea, Grandpa. We'll do that." I patted his hand.

"Supper's on, you two!" Grandma called from the kitchen.

We both got up and walked to the little kitchen table to eat.

CHAPTER 10

$\mathcal{I}$ helped Grandma gather eggs and feed the chickens, goats, and hogs in the morning. Mrs. Colton, Suzy's Mom, had called me to ask if I could give her a hand with something at the museum, and to bring my laptop, so I bathed and changed into a sundress and flats, and headed to town.

At the museum, Mrs. Colton asked me to help her create a poster that could be used for a memorial for Melody. She planned on doing a retrospective of Melody's work the following month, and was getting several local residents to bring in pieces that they owned to showcase in the museum to honor her.

We spent a couple of hours in her office, and in the end, I was happy with the poster we had created. Melody's daughter, Kayla, had provided a photo of her mother that she had taken on a vacation a few years before. Melody had an easel set up on the beach, and wore a long, pale blue tunic and a floppy tan hat in the photo. She painted as the colors of the setting sun washed over her. It was a great photo, and I could see that, even though she didn't paint, Kayla had inherited Melody's artistic eye.

I took another photo of Melody, one from her college days, and used a mosaic-style treatment on it that mimicked her own painting style. We added some images of her work that were on permanent display at the museum, the dates of her life, and the dates of the exhibition. We were both happy with the end result.

After we finished the poster, Mrs. Colton and I sat in her office for a while, chatting over a cup of tea. Mrs. Colton kept an electric tea kettle in the museum's little kitchen, but she had real teacups and saucers in which tea was served. That was how she had always done things: properly. We talked about Suzy's upcoming wedding, and how she was fussing over every detail.

"She is so happy you're back home, Emma. I think she felt like she was missing something while you were gone, and didn't realize what it was until you came back," Mrs. Colton said, patting my shoulder. Mrs. Colton was always kind and warm to me, and her home was always open to me after my parents died.

"I've missed her too," I said, looking down at my teacup. "I always wanted to get out and see the world...and don't get me wrong, New York was great. But, I don't think it hit me how much I missed home until I got here." I wondered if she had any thoughts about Melody's death, or the robbery, for that matter. "It's a bit different, though, you know? I mean, I don't ever remember there being a robbery while we were growing up. Not to mention what happened with poor Melody," I said.

"Oh, yes, well...these are different times, aren't they? The Flower Festival does attract a crowd, and where there are tourists, there are criminals. I told you the story of how Melody's father and I were pickpocketed our first night in

Venice, didn't I?" She shook her head remembering the unpleasantness, and I told her I remembered the story. "At any rate, that's just what happens. Melody's death, though… I'm not sure what you mean. Tucker said it was an accident."

I shook my head and put my cup down on its saucer delicately. "I don't know, Mrs. Colton, I'm not so sure. I know what Tucker said, but I stopped by the spot where she was struck. She was walking so far away from the road it just looked…intentional to me. Do you think anyone would want to hurt her?"

"*Hmpf!* Well, she could be a bit of a mean old biddy if I'm honest. I know, you're not supposed to speak ill of the dead, but if she could hear me right now, I'd be saying the same exact thing!"

She might hear you, I thought, *and if she does, I'm sure I'll hear all about it later.*

"She was just very eccentric, you know? And she and that sister of hers went round and round."

"I'd heard that. Something about a man they both liked, I think. What was all that about, exactly?" My mind went back to the photos at Melody's – the ones from which she had cut Cadence completely.

"Well, you'll notice that Cadence and Melody both go by Campbell. Neither of them ever married. They both fell for the same man, some artist they met at some festival or other, and Cadence thought she would run off with him. She went to go tell him she was coming with him, and overheard him talking to Melody." Mrs. Colton didn't know it, but she was confirming the story I had heard from Grandma. "Anyway, Melody told him she was pregnant with his child, but didn't want anything from him, and was going home to raise her baby."

"How awful for Cadence," I said. "Even if Melody didn't

know she was in a relationship with the same man Cadence loved, how incredibly hurt she must have been."

"Exactly! Melody was always the prettier sister – the one who got more attention. Cadence had always held a bit of a grudge about it. I think that losing the man she had wanted for herself was too much. Not to mention that she had to see Kayla every day, growing up. She must've lived with that hurt every day of her life."

"Wow, you're right! How terrible!" I said, taking one final sip from my cup before returning it to the saucer.

"The Campbells weren't wealthy, but they left the sisters with the house Melody lived in, free and clear, plus there was some money split between them, but not much to live on without additional income of some sort. Melody made good money with her artwork, so she was pretty comfortable. Cadence didn't have her sister's skills, so it was very different for her. Poor dear."

Mrs. Colton shook her head. "Anyway, I'm sure you don't want to sit here all afternoon and listen to old town gossip! Thank you again for your help. I'll be sure you get credit for the work on the website, too. Do stop by and see me again soon, dear, won't you? I've enjoyed our little chat today." She stood and hugged me.

"Thanks, Mrs. Colton. I have too." I hugged her neck tightly, enjoying the motherly embrace.

"And who knows? Maybe after we get Suzy's wedding behind us, we can start planning one for you too?" She winked at me.

"Um, I appreciate the sentiment, Mrs. Colton, but I'm single. Very single, in fact, and Hillbilly Hollow is hardly teaming with eligible bachelors." I laughed.

"Well, there are a few eligible bachelors. I can think of a tall, dark, and handsome one who's been crazy about you since you were kids, in fact. You never know, Emma. Sometimes the very thing you've been looking for is right in front of you. You just can't see it until you shift your focus." She kissed me on top of the head, and I rolled my eyes.

"Oh my goodness, Mrs. C! I can see where Suzy gets it from." I laughed and told her I'd see her soon.

* * *

I WENT over to Suzy's shop to say hi. It was usually pretty quiet on a weekday afternoon, but this particular afternoon, The Posh Closet was hopping with people. When I walked in, I saw Phoebe, the young woman who helped Suzy part-time, at the cash register, and Suzy at the back toward the dressing rooms. I stopped at the cash register, and shoved my purse on a shelf behind the counter.

"Hi, Phoebe," I said quickly as I walked past her.

She gave me an overwhelmed look and a tenuous smile.

I walked back to the dressing rooms. "How can I help?" I asked Suzy.

"Emma! Thank my lucky stars! Those two dressing rooms are empty – can you grab the clothes out and hang them up? Then maybe answer questions on the sales floor? You're a lifesaver!" She looked at me with an expression of incredible gratitude.

I grabbed the clothes from the empty dressing rooms, quickly putting them back on hangers and figuring out where they should go, or at least getting close, and putting them back on the racks. I walked around and made small talk with several of the ladies who were milling around.

A tour company in Branson had apparently started doing a tour that included a stop at the Flower Festival. The tour, called *MO Summer!,* included stops at some of the quaint French-settled villages in the area, and during the week of the Flower Festival, as well as during Old Fort Days, the tour stopped in our little town as well. It was great for business, but being so new, Suzy was understandably surprised and overwhelmed by the sudden influx of customers.

I spent the next three hours helping out where I could. I showed ladies to dressing rooms, bagged up purchases, and even made a few suggestions that resulted in sales. Never having actually worked in the store before, I was pretty proud of my efforts.

Suzy locked the front door around six o'clock and came over to the cash stand, where I had collapsed onto a little stool behind the counter. Phoebe stood beside me, looking a bit shell-shocked.

"Phoebe, honey, go on home. We can come in a little early tomorrow and clean all this up. You did great today. Thanks for all your hard work!" Suzy rubbed the girl's shoulder appreciatively as she walked toward the back exit, smiling. "She's a good girl, that one. I don't know what I'll do if she goes off to college. There aren't many people I trust with my business, ya know."

"Wow, what a day!" I shook my head as Suzy scooted up onto the counter to sit facing me. "Well, at least you should've made some pretty good money today."

"You aren't kiddin'!" Suzy exclaimed. "Now that I know about that tour, I'll call the tour company and get the schedule. I might even offer the drivers a little something for dropping the tour participants at the corner nearest my door. Maybe work with Sweet Adeline's and do some cooperative advertising." For a small-town girl, Suzy had a real head for business. She loved her little shop, and had always loved clothes, but she was definitely working with the intention of turning a profit.

"That sounds like a great idea. Let me know if you need help with flyers or anything. If I'm honest, I don't have quite enough to do, so I could use the project, even though I'd never charge you," I replied. "Speaking of, I spent the afternoon with your mom. We finished the flyer for the memorial exhibition for Melody."

"Oh yeah? She said you were coming by. Speaking of... any more ideas about what happened to Melody?" Suzy asked. "I know how you think, Emma, and I'm sure something has to be rattling around in that big brain of yours."

"Well, it seems like there are at least three people who had a serious beef with her at the time she died. Dr. Langston could not have been happy that she was suing him for wrongful death of her dog," I said.

"Oh, good grief! That dog was sixteen, at least! That was not his fault," Suzy said. "Still, Melody never went anywhere without him. She loved that dog better than most people."

"Right! Then there's Jennie Weaver. She almost got fired thanks to Melody's complaints. I don't know if a young girl like her is capable of murder, but I hear that her boyfriend is pretty sketchy. Dylan, I think his name is." I looked at Suzy who was thoughtful.

"You know, I could kind of see that, I guess. Those folks up at Happy Hills are sort of a tight-knit group. You mess with one of them, you get them all, sorta thing, you know? In fact, I think I know who Dylan is. He hasn't been in town all that long. I think he moved here about four or five years ago. He worked up at the dog food plant, and I think some folks from Happy Hills told him it was cheap to live here, so he moved in. I could definitely see him being trouble." Suzy nodded as if convincing herself this was a likely option.

"The last person I've heard a lot about is Cadence," I said. "She and Melody had a beef going back years, from what I hear."

"She is really strange, too, Emma. I mean, she has lived all alone on the cemetery grounds for years. I see her when we go up to change out the flowers on the Bailey plots, and she kind of gives me the creeps." Suzy shuddered as she said the last phrase.

"I hear that the father of Melody's daughter, Kayla, was a man that Cadence was in love with. That can't have made for a good relationship between the two," I replied.

"No, definitely not." Suzy crossed her arms and put her index finger to her chin, tapping it lightly. "So, the three people with a real grudge against Melody seem to be Dr. Langston, Jennie Weaver, and by extension, her boyfriend Dylan, and Cadence Campbell...but did any of them hate her enough to kill her?" Suzy asked.

"That's what we have to figure out. I need to find so much evidence pointing toward the real killer that when I take it to Tucker, he can't help but listen," I replied.

"Oh geez! Look at the time. I better get home. Brian's coming over and we're supposed to be going over the guest list. Again!" She laughed. "Don't get me wrong – it's a good problem to have, but the venue only holds so many people."

"As long as I'm on the list," I replied with a smile, grabbing my handbag.

"I've been meaning to talk to you about that, actually..." Suzy said, sheepishly.

"Uh-oh. What's up?" I replied.

"Well, do you think...would you be willing to be my maid of honor?" she asked.

"What? Would I! I would be so honored, Suzy!" I threw my arms around her neck, hugging her close, and she returned the tight embrace.

"I'm so happy! And I promise, no hideous dresses!" She laughed. "Brian has two groomsmen – his best man is his brother Brad, and he's going to have Billy as his other groomsman. That was for me, really. My cousin Penelope will be my other bridesmaid."

We hugged again, and Suzy locked the front door behind

us as we left. As I got to my truck, my phone buzzed. It was a text from Billy.

BILLY: U still in town?

    ME: How did u know im in town? Stalker!

    BILLY: Can u come 2 dinner?

    ME: It's pretty late - should get home

Billy sent me a picture of Halee with the word "PLEASE" underneath it.

    ME: Man u play dirty. B there in 15

I CALLED my Grandma on the way to Billy's. She was fine with me staying out for dinner.

She loved Billy like family, and never worried if I was with him or Suzy.

hen I knocked on Billy's front door, I could immediately hear the familiar sound of little nails scratching on hardwood floors coming from the other side.

"Hi, Emma!" Billy said as he answered the door. Halee was beside him, jumping up and down for me to pick her up.

"Hi there," I said, as I bent down to pick up the little dog I had grown so fond of. She leaned up and deposited puppy kisses on my cheek as I held her and walked inside.

"I can do steaks or fish – your choice," Billy said as he led me to the kitchen.

"Either is fine – whatever is easier for you to grill. Or should I say faster? I'm pretty hungry!" I laughed.

"Okay, fish it is." He smiled, grabbing the plate of fish from the refrigerator. "Can you grab those ears of corn for me?"

I followed him outside to the grill.

Billy got busy firing up the grill and I made myself at home on one of the lounge chairs with Halee in my lap. After getting the fish started, Billy disappeared back into the house, returning with a bowl of salad and a couple of cans of soda. He sat down on the lounge chair next to mine and handed me one of the cans.

"So, how's the investigation going?" he asked nonchalantly.

I sighed. "Suzy has such a big mouth."

He laughed. "She does, but we love her anyway. Besides, I don't think we could get rid of her now if we tried." He smiled at me, raising an eyebrow playfully.

I looked over at Billy as he relaxed back on the chair, his eyes closed, and one arm raised above his head, the band of his polo shirt sleeve straining to contain his muscular arm. He had a strong jawline, and raven black hair. I thought about what Mrs. Colton had said. He certainly would be a great catch for someone.

"Emma, why are you staring at me? It's creepy."

"I wasn't staring!" I lied. "Besides, you're the one who knows what I'm doing with your eyes shut. Now *that's* creepy." I laughed.

"I think you're trying to avoid the subject. I know you haven't let go of this whole thing with Melody. What did you find out?" he said, sitting up again.

"Well, I was just talking to Suzy before I came over. We have it narrowed down to three people who had a serious beef with Melody," I said, scratching Halee on the head.

"Oh yeah? You were asking me an awful lot about Jerry Langston. Is he on your list?" Billy asked.

"As a matter of fact, he is. Did you know Melody was suing him?" I asked, feeling superior about my sleuthing skills.

"Jerry told you that?" Billy asked.

"Nope, I found the letter from the attorney," I replied quickly, then realized my mistake at divulging this bit of information.

"*Found* it? Emma! What did you do?" Billy had reverted to his authoritative voice – his doctor voice.

"I just…I was looking around a little, and…" I started, but he cut me off.

"Did you break into Melody's house?"

"I didn't break in! I had permission!" I said defiantly.

"Emma, you can't get permission from dead people. Do you know how that would have sounded if someone had caught you there? Even your *good friend* Tucker couldn't look the other way if he had found you at her house. Promise me you won't do that again." He leaned forward, his dark eyes serious beneath his full, dark brows.

"I promise. You're right. I wasn't thinking," I replied.

"Besides all of the laws you broke, I don't think Jerry is capable of hurting anyone." He got up and tended to the grill.

"Maybe not," I said, "but I overheard him telling his wife he had taken care of the Melody problem. That sounded kind of suspicious. But he's not my only suspect."

Billy chuckled. "Okay, who else is on your list?"

"Are you mocking me?" I asked playfully. "He's mocking me, Halee. What do you think of that?"

The pup rolled over onto all fours, and put her paws on my chest, her little tail wagging as she tried to get close to my face.

"At any rate," I continued, "there's also Jennie Weaver. Melody got her in hot water at work, and I hear her boyfriend is a little on the rough side. I've also heard some crazy stuff about Cadence Campbell. How about you? What do you think?"

"I don't know," Billy said as he pulled the food from the grill. "Food's ready." He held the plate up and walked toward the outdoor table.

I sat up and put Halee on the ground, and joined him at the table.

"I mean, you've been around more than I have – you know these people. Plus you saw the accident scene. You don't have a thought about who might have killed Melody?" I asked, helping myself to a piece of salmon, and an ear of corn.

"Well, I don't know. I don't know Dylan Shepherd very well, but I've heard he runs with a rough crowd, and those folks up at Happy Hills seem to really hold grudges. If Jennie got in trouble on account of Melody…he might have taken things too far. One thing though, I'm not sure he has anything other than a motorcycle," Billy said, holding out a portion of salad between the serving forks to put some on my plate.

"Oh, that's a good point!" I exclaimed. "You are right, of course. I suppose he could've borrowed a truck, but that seems like a lot of coincidences all lining up at once. Hmm." I took a bite of my salmon. "Wow, Billy, this is delicious! You're such a good cook!"

"Thanks," he said, a faint hue of pink coming into his cheeks. "I'm glad you like it."

"Mrs. Colton was right. You really are a…" I stopped myself, realizing I hadn't meant to say it out loud.

"I'm sorry, I'm a what was that now?" Billy asked, grinning broadly.

My cheeks burned, betraying the shade of crimson they had turned. "I…um…I saw Mrs. Colton today, and she started talking about you. She said you were a real catch." I never could lie to him or Suzy – there was no point in trying to start now.

Billy laughed. "Well, I'm glad *someone* seems to think so. I'm not sure Mrs. Colton is my type, though, not to mention the existence of Mr. Colton being a real sticking point."

"*And* you'd be Suzy's dad. How weird would *that* be?" I laughed, but was still embarrassed.

"Yeah, that's gonna be a hard pass for me, I'm afraid," he said, still chuckling.

We finished dinner, and I helped him put away the dishes. We sat outside for a little while, chatting, and I decided I had better get home when I realized it was getting pretty late. I gave Halee a little squeeze and deposited her on the lounge chair before standing up. Billy stood up quickly, and as I started to turn, he grabbed my arm.

"Emma, you look really great, ya know," he said.

"That was random, but thanks." I smiled, feeling a bit awkward.

"I mean, since you've been home...I know you came back because of what happened in New York – the accident. It seems like since you've been here, though, you've really done well. You have a sort of, I don't know, glow about you. Like you feel really good. I feel like I have the old Emma back." He gave me a little smirk.

"Oh. Yeah, I mean, I see what you're talking about. It was a little awkward at first, but now, I feel better being here. I feel at home again. And I didn't realize how much I missed you guys until I got back. Oh! Speaking of..." I had suddenly remembered my conversation with Suzy. "Suzy asked me to be her maid of honor."

"That's great, Emma! She's been wanting to ask you for a while. We're all really glad you're back."

I patted his shoulder, and grabbed my bag off the chair, turning to leave.

"Wait," Billy said, and when I turned around, he had one hand on his hip, his head was bent forward, and he was rubbing his temples with his thumb and forefinger. "There's something else. I asked you to come to dinner because there was something I wanted to ask you," he said hesitantly.

"Anything! What is it?" I stepped back toward him.

"I-I need a date," he blurted.

"Oh. Well…I mean, we literally know all the same people, but if you're asking me to set you up with somebody, I guess I can give it a try." I wasn't sure what he meant, and was equally unsure why the idea of setting him up with someone made a knot form in the pit of my stomach.

"Huh? No, no, Emma, that's not what I meant." He chuckled. "No, I need a date for this thing I have to go to in Springfield. It's a dinner for the Missouri Rural Physician's Association. I published a paper examining recent findings on mineral deficits in patients who have fluoridated city water versus those on spring and well systems. It's painfully boring to anyone who's not in the medical profession, but the association is recognizing me for the work. I just found out that I'm expected to bring a plus one. I was hoping to take someone I could enjoy spending the evening with to make it less boring."

"So you want me to help you figure out who to take?" I asked, still unclear on what was happening.

"No. No! I…" He sighed and shook his head. "I suck at this. I want you. I mean, I want you to go with me. To be my date. To the thing." He rubbed his face with both palms and looked up, placing both hands on his waist before turning his gaze back to me. "Please Emma, will you be my date to the dinner?"

"Oh!" I exclaimed, feeling a wave of relief wash over me when I realized he was not asking me to set him up. "Of course, I'll go with you. When is it?"

"Friday night. Sorry – short notice, I know. And it's black tie. Do you have something to wear? I don't want you to have to buy something on my account. If you need a dress, I can…" his demeanor was apologetic as he rubbed a palm on the back of his neck.

"It's fine," I said, putting my palm on his chest in a calming gesture. "I'm sure I have something, and if I don't

Suzy can hook me up. No problem. What time do I need to be ready? Should I just come here?" I asked.

"No, no. I'll come to pick you up. How about five-thirty? It will take us about an hour to get into the city, and the dinner starts at seven." He smiled, seeming relieved.

"Sounds good." I smiled back up at him.

"Okay! It's a date!" he said, then toned down his enthusiasm. "I mean, well not a...well, you know it's just an expression."

"Thanks for dinner, Billy," I said, reaching up to put my arms around his neck. He pulled me close as he hugged me, and I leaned against his chest.

"Thanks, Emma," he whispered as he put his cheek to the top of my head.

As I drove back to the farm that night, I thought about the evening. Billy and I had always flirted a little. He was my oldest friend, though, and the idea of going out with him outside of the cocoon of our little hometown felt strange. It wasn't a date – not a real one. Still, for some reason, all the way home, I couldn't stop smiling at the thought of our night out in the city.

It was almost enough to make me forget about the ghost of Melody Campbell – for a while.

CHAPTER 12

I spent the following day doing chores around the farm with Grandpa, and looking forward to my night out in civilization, or at least as close to civilization as I could get within an hour of Hillbilly Hollow. Some of the spring calves were ready for branding and there were a few that needed to be banded. It was an unpleasant task, but a necessary one on a cattle farm.

Tending to livestock was an arduous, exhausting process. Not only did it involve climbing over fences, chasing animals down, and leading large, strong, heavy creatures around pens to get them where you wanted them, it could be dangerous, too. I remembered the goat that had kicked me in the ribs a few months before. I had been pretty lucky, honestly. It could have cracked a rib, and I could've ended up with a pierced lung. For that matter, its hooves could've gotten me in the face. I remembered being in middle school when Shane Phillips had to miss a week of school after being kicked by a foal. The horse had connected with his face at just the right angle to shatter his cheekbone, break his nose, and knock out two teeth. He had been standing in the wrong place when the

97

foal got nervous and began to buck. It was a lesson I had tried never to forget.

I spent the late afternoon doing some graphic design work I had picked up from a freelancing site. I created a couple of logos, and did a flyer for a bakery. I poured a lot of care and effort into each job. Although they didn't pay much, each one garnered me good reviews on the freelancing site, and I knew I'd soon be able to raise my rates. I also spent some time reaching out to former colleagues via a business networking site, to let them know I was doing some virtual freelancing in hopes of getting some additional business.

I had decided to sublet my space in New York, and wasn't going to renew when the lease came up in the fall. I had put all my belongings in storage and would return to get them in a month or two. I could get rid of some furniture and house-hold items, and store what I needed to in one of the outbuildings on the farm. I wished I had done it sooner, actually, given that I needed something nice to wear for my evening out in Springfield. Still, Suzy was going to help me pick out something from her shop the following morning, and I had a pair of nice heels I could wear. A New Yorker never travels without a pair of heels – even if she's a transplant.

After I finished working, I went downstairs and had dinner with my grandparents. We spent the evening watching retro television. They would never have paid for cable themselves, but I knew Grandma and Grandpa were happy to have some more of their favorite programs to watch. When one about a psychic who saw ghosts came on, I had to chuckle.

"Oh look, Emma! You should like this one," Grandma said, patting my knee.

When I had told them about my newfound abilities, Grandma and Grandpa had shared that both Grandpa's cousin and his father had similar experiences after a blow to the head. Apparently my ability to see spirits was something of a family tradition.

"I wonder if the person who wrote this show knew someone in our family." I chuckled, and Grandpa gave a wry smile.

"You never know," Grandpa replied.

I was worn out from a full day on the farm plus an afternoon full of working on the computer. I took a hot bath to help me relax, and got dressed in my night clothes before heading out to the outhouse to get ready for bed. I pulled on my muck boots, and Snowball followed me past the garden and out to the little building at the edge of the wood. I brushed my teeth and used the toilet. As I stepped on the flusher, I heard a sound behind me like someone clearing their throat. I whipped around to find Melody standing before me.

"Sugar! You scared the pants off of me!" I exclaimed. "What are you doing in *here*?" I asked.

"I came to talk to you, obviously!" she said.

"Were you standing there while I was using the bathroom? That's disgusting! AND a huge invasion of my privacy!" I said angrily, crossing my arms.

"Emma, I'm dead! If I did see something, who am I going to tell about it? You're the only one who can see me, remember?" She rolled her eyes exaggeratedly.

I stomped my foot down on the flusher again, and went to wash my hands. "Could you step aside, please?" I asked.

"Why? I'm not in your way – not really. Just step forward," Melody replied. I did, and was able to step right through her. It was cooler in the space she was occupying, and felt a bit like standing in the middle of a heavy fog.

"That's creepy!" I said. "Can we take this conversation outside, please?"

"Fine!" she exclaimed, and disappeared through the still closed door.

I stepped out of the outhouse and shut the door, closing the latch to keep out any unwanted animal visitors. Melody was floating just above the ground in front of me, next to where Snowball was lying in a cool grassy spot. She looked up at the apparition and gave a short bleat before resting her head lazily back on the cool grass.

"So, to what do I owe the pleasure?" I asked Melody.

"I came to see how you're doing. I'm still here, so I take it you haven't found my killer," she said smugly.

"As a matter of fact, I have three very solid suspects! I need to ask you about something, though," I replied, remembering the banner.

"What's that?"

"The banner – the one you painted for the Flower Festival auction. I bought it for my Grandma, but someone stole it from our front porch, and burned it. Any idea who would've done that?" I asked.

"Well, seeing as how I didn't paint a banner this year, I've no idea what you're talking about," she replied.

"What do you mean? You did paint a banner – I bought it," I said.

"No ma'am – I did not. I ran out of time, and told Jackie Colton I'd paint a new, permanent piece for the museum instead," she replied.

"Hmm…the banner I bought had *M. Campbell* in the bottom, right-hand corner, and it was definitely painted in your style." I thought for a moment, and realized I had my phone in the pocket of my shirt. "Oh, here, I have a photo of it." I pulled up the image I had taken of Grandma standing in front of the banner, and zoomed in.

"Oh, I see," Melody replied. "I see where you would be confused. That's not mine – it's Mel's."

"Mel? Mel who?" I asked. "Is someone copying your work?"

"Not exactly. Mel is my granddaughter. Kayla's child. She's an artist, just like her granny." Melody leaned back, raising her chin proudly. "She was old enough to enter a piece this year. It's a twelve-and-up category. She must've entered one. That's not like her usual work, though," Melody said, looking back toward the phone. "It's a little dark for her."

"I thought it was a little…I don't know…something as well. Do you have any idea what is depicted in the painting? It looks so familiar but I can't quite place it," I said.

"Hmm…" She thought for a moment. "Oh, I know! It could be…"

Suddenly she disappeared.

I turned around to see Grandma traipsing up the path to the outhouse.

"Everything alright, Emma dear?" she asked sweetly. She had on her dressing gown and boots.

"Yes, Grandma. Just getting ready for bed," I said.

"Me too," she replied. "Sleep well, my girl."

"You too, Grandma." I patted my leg to call Snowball, and headed back to the house.

Well, Sugar! Melody was just about to tell me what was in the painting. I hoped she would be back soon to help me make sense of it.

There were no other signs of Melody that evening. I lay in bed and as colored shapes flashed in mosaics in my mind, I drifted off to sleep.

CHAPTER 13

I was a little taken aback when Billy told me to pack a bag to take with us to Springfield. He explained, though, that the after dinner reception might go late, and since the conference had gotten him a room at the hotel where the event was being held, he had called and booked a second room for me as well. I threw some jeans, a couple of tops, and a few essentials in the smaller of the two suitcases I had brought with me when I first came home from New York.

When I stopped by Suzy's shop, she had already set up a dressing room with several cocktail dresses for me. A couple of them were a bit young for my taste.

"Cocktail dresses, prom dresses, potato, po-tah-to," Suzy dismissed.

I had brought my heels so I could see how they looked properly. I settled on a sapphire blue dress that was conservative in the front, with a high neckline. It had a slit up the side to just above the knee to allow movement since the straight skirt went almost to the ankle. The back had a little dip to just above the bottom of my shoulder blades. I had to admit, I felt really glamorous when I put it on. I opened the door to the dressing room, and stepped out to find both Suzy and Phoebe waiting for me.

"Oh, my!" Suzy exclaimed when she saw me. "Emma you are – well, you're just stunning!" Phoebe didn't say anything but simply nodded, her mouth agape. They had never seen me in anything but jeans or sundresses, after all, so I was sure seeing me dressed up was a shock.

"Ooh – and I have the perfect clutch for it," Suzy said, running to the case of handbags and accessories beside the register. She returned with a small, black clutch that had a small, pretty design along the clasp in crystals.

"I think this is the one," I said, looking at myself in the three-way mirror.

Suzy grabbed her phone and started texting.

"What are you doing?" I asked.

"Hmm? Oh! Nothing. Just…nothing. Okay, let's get this hung back up. You need to get home and start your ritual," she said.

"What ritual?" I asked.

"You know – the *ritual*. Whatever you do when you're getting all dolled up to go out. Put on some music, take a bath, paint your nails…you know. The ritual!" She smiled broadly and raised an eyebrow.

"Oh, right! Yeah, I guess I do."

Of course I had done all those things when I lived in the city. It felt like ages since I had been out on a date, or out with girlfriends for a night on the town, so I hoped I wasn't so rusty that I'd forgotten how to get really done up. This wasn't a date, after all. I was going out with one of my best friends as a favor. Still, I wanted to look nice – for him to feel good about having me on his arm when he was there with all his doctor friends.

* * *

I WENT HOME, and within a couple of hours, the ritual was complete. I had curled my hair into loose waves, and went with minimal makeup, punctuated by high-drama lashes and lips. As I put on my makeup, it occurred to me that Billy was right. I did look more relaxed – healthier than I had when I first got back to town.

I had dropped my overnight bag in the living room, and only had to put my toiletries kit in the top when I came downstairs.

"Oh my *stars!*" Grandma exclaimed. "Ed! Come quick! Look at our girl!"

"Grandma, stop it! It's still me!" I said, giggling a little.

"Well, I'll be," Grandpa said quietly when he came out from the bedroom. "She looks just like her, don't she?" He shook his head.

"She does, Ed. As I live and breathe, she does," Grandma replied as he put an arm around her shoulders.

I didn't have to ask. I knew they were talking about my mom. I could see from the pictures I had of my parents that I looked more like her all the time. She wasn't much older than I was now when she died. I touched the back of my index finger to my bottom lashes.

"Stop it, you two! I worked really hard on my makeup and you're going to ruin it," I said playfully.

"Oh, wait! I know just the thing!" Grandma said, running into the bedroom and returning with a small, velvet box. "Put these on. They're perfect! You should have them anyway."

She opened the box to reveal a pair of the most beautiful, art nouveau diamond earrings I had ever seen. My gasp upon seeing them was audible.

"Grandma! They're stunning! Where did they come

from?" I asked, carefully taking one and then the other from the box and putting them on.

"They were your Great-Grandma's. Your mother wore them on her wedding day. They look as beautiful on you as they did on her, honey." She leaned forward, kissing me on the forehead.

"Thanks, Grandma," I said, air-kissing her cheek so as not to get lipstick on her.

There was a knock at the front door, and Grandpa let in Billy, who had a bouquet of flowers in his hand.

"Wow, are those for me?" I asked.

When he saw me, Billy smiled immediately, and so did I. He had on a charcoal suit that fit him perfectly.

"Actually, no, they're for Mrs. Hooper," he said, handing Grandma the flowers. "I heard your banner was stolen, so I wanted to bring you something to brighten your day."

Grandpa turned to Billy, shook his hand, and patted him on the shoulder.

"I suppose we should get going," Billy said, grabbing my overnight bag in one hand, and putting the elbow of his other arm out for me to take. I was surprised to see a flashy convertible sitting in front of our house as we stepped outside.

"What happened to your truck?" I asked, expecting his SUV.

"Oh, I thought this would be more comfortable. I only drive it in the summer – I keep it in the garage." He opened the passenger door for me, and I waved goodbye to my grandparents, who were standing on the front porch. Billy put my bag in the trunk, then took off his jacket, hanging it in the backseat before getting in the car.

The drive to Springfield took about an hour. The weather was nice, and we cranked up the radio, playing some old school 90s music as we drove.

The hotel was in the oldest part of the city, surrounded by historic buildings and landmarks. Billy gave his key to the valet when we arrived, and pulled his jacket from the hanger in the backseat, slipping it on as he got out of the car. When he opened the passenger door, I was careful to swing my legs around and plant my feet securely before standing so as to not trip over the long hem of my dress.

Billy put his elbow out and I hooked my arm in his as we walked inside. He leaned down as we walked through the lobby and said, "You look absolutely stunning. Thanks for coming with me, Emma."

I felt the blush rise in my cheeks. It was me who should have been thanking him. The hotel was gorgeous, and the ballroom was set up for a beautiful dinner.

The room was quickly filling up as we arrived, and Billy introduced me to several doctors who were on the state board, and a few who he knew from med school. Dinner seating was assigned, and we were at one of the front tables, closest to the stage. We sat with a few older doctors and their respective spouses, all of whom were friendly. A couple of them, like Billy, were slated to speak after dinner. The food was delicious – just what one would expect from a high-end hotel.

As the evening drew to a close, the emcee announced that the final speaker was the winner of the year's most prestigious state-wide award, and announced Billy as Dr. Will Stone. The whole crowd erupted with applause. I was so happy for Billy, and proud that he had asked me to be there.

Billy gave his speech on mineral absorption and water sources. I didn't quite follow all of it – many of the terms were highly technical, but it was well-received and he got a standing ovation when he was finished.

After dinner, we mingled at the cocktail hour. "Oh, I see the person I wanted you to meet," Billy said looking past my shoulder. "Come on." He grabbed me by the hand and led me over to a group of men standing by the bar.

"Dr. Edelson," Billy said when the men's conversation lulled, "I wanted you to meet Emma Hooper. We spoke briefly about Emma's injuries. Emma," he said, turning to me, "Dr. Edelson is a highly-respected neurologist. He specializes in closed traumatic brain injuries like the one you had."

"So nice to meet you," I said, sticking out my hand and wondering why Billy wanted me to meet this particular person. My head had healed, after all, save the occasional ghost sighting.

"Gentlemen, if you'll excuse us," Edelson said to the other men, then he led Billy and me to a door at the back of the room that led to a quiet patio.

"So, Ms. Hooper. Will tells me you had a closed brain injury, and have experienced associated audio-visual phenomena ever since. Is that right?" the doctor asked.

"Yes," I said, casting a disappointed glance at Billy. I couldn't believe that he would share something so personal that I had told him in confidence.

"Listen, please don't be cross with Will." He looked at Billy. "I have been doing research on this very subject for over twenty years. He heard me speak at a conference, and when we started talking afterward, I saw his face when I spoke about my findings. I knew he had someone in his life that had this injury – someone very important to him, and so I drug it out of him."

Billy dropped his arms and looked down, embarrassed. I knew he was trying to help. If nothing else, I always knew I could count on him. I tucked my arm through his elbow and patted him gently. He looked up, and I felt his whole body yield as a sigh of relief escaped him.

"So, young lady, may I ask you a few questions?"

I nodded my head, and Edelson asked me about the accident, how long I was in the hospital, and about the manifestation of the visions I had been having. As soon as I answered him, he began nodding. "Yes, yes! That's exactly as I thought."

"One other thing," I added. "I recently found out that a couple of other family members – my great-uncle and great grandfather – had similar injuries and also had the visions afterwards. Is that significant?"

"That's very interesting, actually," Dr. Edelson said. "I have seen cases where multiple family members had similar experiences, but not across such broad generations. But you know, my dear, the thing I want you to remember is that not everything can be fully quantified in science. I can measure and study hundreds and thousands of cases, but yours may be unique. You may wake up tomorrow, and never have another vision. On the other hand, you could have them the rest of your life. The important thing for you to remember is that either case is absolutely fine. You are still a bright, healthy, vibrant young woman. These visions will only take over as much of your life as you let them. Besides, who is to say we know everything? Perhaps there is something – some connection – that is open to you that the rest of us simply cannot see. There was a time when the symptoms of wisdom teeth were mistaken for madness, and there was no understanding of the existence of germs. Who knows what science will discover tomorrow that is wholly unseen today."

I felt strangely comforted after our talk. Dr. Edelson excused himself, and left me alone on the balcony with Billy. He seemed nervous. "Are you very angry with me, Emma?" he asked, his dark eyes looking up at me from under his brows.

"No, of course not. I was a little worried at first," I said, gently touching my fingertips to his arm. "I didn't know why you were having me talk with him. Then when Dr. Edelson started explaining his work...I feel so much better now." A look of profound relief crossed Billy's face.

"I'm so glad!" He blew out a deep breath. "I was worried you'd be upset."

"No, I can't stay angry at you. You know that. Besides, I know you were trying to help me. I know you care about me." I smiled up at him, and he wrapped his arms around me.

"I really do, Emma."

We called it a night and went up to our rooms. As we got to the doors of the adjoining suites, Billy handed me my room key.

"Oh, and Emma? I hope you don't mind, but I did something kinda crazy."

"Uh-oh...what's that then?" I asked nervously.

He leaned in and whispered, "I requested late checkout, so we can sleep in as late as we want!" He planted a kiss on my cheek. "Thanks again for coming with me. Goodnight, Emma."

"Goodnight Billy. Oh and one other thing?"

"Hmm? What's that?" he asked.

"Your work – your speech – you were really impressive tonight. I'm really proud of you." I leaned up and kissed him on the cheek. "Goodnight, Billy."

His cheeks filled with crimson, and the smile that crept across his face made me incredibly happy.

* * *

INSIDE MY ROOM, I closed the blackout curtains, washed my face, changed into a nightshirt, and collapsed into the most comfortable bed I had slept in in months.

I was grateful for Billy's idea about late checkout, and

slept so hard it was like I was sedated. When I finally rolled over the following morning, it was nine-thirty. I laughed right out loud.

At home, this would never do! If you sleep this late on the farm, you better have the plague!

I took a luxurious, hot shower in the spacious hotel bathroom, and put on the jeans and top I had brought for the drive home. I texted Billy as I was putting the finishing touches on my makeup, and we met in the hallway thirty minutes later.

"Sleep well?" he asked.

"Like I haven't slept in ages! How about you?" I asked.

"Really well, thanks. You were such a hit last night. Everyone loved you. All my colleagues think I'm cool now, having shown up to this event with the prettiest woman in Missouri." He winked at me playfully.

"Billy Stone! Are you trying to butter me up for something?" I laughed.

"As a matter of fact, I am. There's a fundraiser in November, so I thought I should start getting on your good side now so you'll come to that too." He grinned. "And now, I'm really going to earn some brownie points...I'm taking you to the best brunch in town."

WELL-RESTED AND WITH FULL BELLIES, we headed back to Hillbilly Hollow. We talked on the drive home about the conference, and I thanked Billy again for having me talk with Dr. Edelson. I couldn't quite explain it, but even though I had talked to Jenson back in New York for months – he was the one who had suggested I come home, after all – I felt so much better hearing from a neurologist that my experience was completely valid, and might get better, or not, but in either case, I would be okay.

As we got onto the main highway into town, the traffic app alarmed. Looking at his phone, Billy saw a huge backup. He quickly dialed the Sherriff's department. They told him that a transport truck full of chickens had taken the curve along the highway too fast, and tipped over. No one was hurt, but they were having a heck of a time rounding up the chickens, and it was causing a major backup.

"Okay, looks like we have to take the alternate route," Billy said, turning off the highway and onto the old state road. We drove along twists and turns, getting closer and closer to town. As we came to a stop sign, we were perpendicular to the road that became Main Street in town. That stretch was County Road 47. There was a dog-leg road just up from the one we were on, and I recognized it as the back route to the Hollow Heights Gardens, and knew we were close to Founders Park, and Main Street. There was a small booth that had been constructed as the alternate entrance to the Flower Festival, and cars were stopping at it to pay their entrance fees as they filtered in from the highway. I looked across the street at the small field adjacent to the entrance booth as we sat at the stop sign, and my eyes focused on a small, brick structure.

Suddenly, Mrs. Colton's words popped back into my head. *Sometimes the very thing you've been looking for is right in front of you. You just can't see it until you shift your focus.*

Across the road, rows of brightly colored flowers butted up against the roadway. Behind them, the grass was a dark, rich green. In the small, open field sat a cylindrical structure of stone and brick that I recognized as the old town well. I looked to my right and saw a house on the corner.

"Hey Billy," I said, turning to him, "whose house is that on this side of the road?"

"Oh, I think that's Kayla Greene's place. You know – she was Melody's daughter. Why do you ask?" he said.

"Oh, I was just curious, that's all," I lied.

It all made sense. I was starting to have a hunch about Melody's murderer and I knew exactly where I should investigate next.

CHAPTER 14

*A*s soon as Billy dropped me off at home, I grabbed the keys to the old farm truck and headed to town. There were only two days left in the Flower Festival, and I knew most folks around would be at the Main Street Fair that was going on in town. Anyone with kids would definitely be there, as this was the most family-friendly event of the week. There would be bouncy-houses and face painting, and all sorts of activities for kids. I had a hunch that Kayla Greene would be there as well, with her daughter Melanie in tow.

I parked the truck in back of Suzy's boutique, and headed into the swarm of people. I passed through the activities that were geared toward a younger crowd, and headed for the arts and crafts tent. The tent was full of teens and tweens working on everything from friendship bracelets to embellished t-shirts. Toward the back of the tent, I saw a few girls painting on canvases. Their mothers, and a few of the fathers, were watching over their work with interest. I recognized Kayla right away from the photos on Melody's fridge.

I walked up to her and introduced myself. "Hi, you must be Kayla. I'm Emma Hooper. I don't think we've met." I put my hand out, and she shook it.

"Hi, Emma. Yes, I'm Kayla Greene, and this is my daughter, Mel." She stroked the hair that fell down the girl's back lovingly.

"I am so sorry for the intrusion. I knew your mother, and I just wanted to say how sorry I was to hear about your loss."

"Thank you so much, Emma. It has been hard, especially on Mel. They were really close." She looked at her daughter.

"If it's not too much trouble, I was hoping to ask you about the banner I purchased at the auction. I thought it was one of Melody's, but I understand she didn't submit a banner this year."

I saw the little girl's eyes grow wide, but she stayed quiet.

I said, "Mel, I understand from your Grandma that sometimes you used to paint and use her name – Campbell. Is that right?"

The girl looked sheepishly at me, then to her mother, and back before nodding her head up and down. She seemed afraid to talk.

"I understand. I used to live in New York, and I work in graphic design. I know lots of artists that use a different name on their work. Your painting is excellent, by the way. That was your banner in the auction, wasn't it, Mel?"

The girl nodded again. "Yes, I told Grandma I wanted to submit a banner, so she helped me do it. I wasn't trying to trick anyone. I don't want to get in trouble!"

"Oh, no, of course not. That's just wonderful. I'm so glad she could help you do that. Do you mind if I ask you something else about the banner?"

Mel shook her head no, so I continued.

"That scene that was on the banner, that was the old well, wasn't it?

"It-it is, but I didn't go over there. I didn't. I promise!" she said nervously. The girl was clearly terrified of someone, or something.

"That's okay, Mel. Really, it's alright. Thank you for telling me about your work. I hope I get to buy another one of your pieces someday." I smiled at the girl, and gently touched her shoulder. She gave a small smile back, at least letting me know I hadn't scared her.

"Can I ask what all this is about?" Kayla asked.

"Oh, of course. It's nothing, really. I bought Mel's banner in the auction, for my grandmother. At first, I thought it was one of Melody's, and I think other people did too based on the number of bids it received. Anyway, someone stole it from the front porch of our house, so I guess I just wanted to learn more about it. You know, with it garnering such interest that someone would take it and everything. I didn't mean to disturb you at all," I said gently.

"Oh, no, that's alright. I'm just so sorry someone stole your banner. I hope you find it," Kayla said, patting her daughter on the shoulder. "Come on, Mel, we have to go now. Nice meeting you, Emma," Kayla said.

* * *

I WALKED around downtown for a bit and thought about the situation. In my mind's eye, I pictured the banner again. The slightly impressionist design had depicted brightly colored flowers along the bottom, and a background of medium and dark green tones. Off to the left had been a cylindrical looking shape of dark grays and browns—the old well. And beyond it had been a black shape that looked like a human figure—maybe someone wearing a hood.

I considered the possibility that whoever murdered Melody might have also been the hooded figure who visited the well. If they were hiding something in the well, it must be something pretty important to be worth killing someone over. And Melody's granddaughter, her house had been positioned just right for her to have glimpsed that mysterious person. If she had been too frightened to talk about the figure she had seen at the well, what could be more natural than to have shown it in her picture instead?

I went home and waited for nightfall to return to the well and see what I could figure out. There were security cameras on the small hut that was used to take entrance fees to the festival, but when I pulled off the highway up the road from the well, I could see that they couldn't possibly capture the entire field based on their angle. The crumbling well looked incredibly dangerous on its own without the intervention of a murderer.

I shone my flashlight down into the dark pit, and couldn't see anything except the ancient rope that held the bucket. I carefully pulled the bucket up from the depths. It looked like it had rarely been moved in decades, and I was afraid that the rope might give way, sending the whole thing crashing to the bottom of the well.

As the bucket neared the surface, I could see it contained some sort of package. I held the small flashlight between my teeth to get a better view. When I finally hauled the bucket up, carefully leaning over the decaying stone to reach it, I immediately saw that it was a large, plastic zipper bag, the kind people use to put food in their freezer. Inside of that was another bag – a white grocery-style bag that bore a familiar logo: *Chapman's Market.*

I pulled the package from the bucket, and lowered the bucket back into the well, and took the plastic bag back to the truck. Once inside, I turned on the interior lights and examined the bag carefully. I still had a couple of pair of rubber gloves in the truck from my adventure at Melody's, so

THE GHASTLY GHOST OF HILLBILLY HOLLOW

I put some on before I opened the bag. I may not have been a professional detective, but I had seen enough crime shows to know I shouldn't be putting my fingerprints on evidence.

When I pulled the top of the bag apart, and opened the white grocery bag inside, the very thing I expected to find came into view. Dozens of banded stacks of cash were in the bag – thousands of dollars' worth at least. It was definitely the money from the gas station robbery. I quickly bundled the money back up, and fired off a text to Tucker, asking him to meet me at his office right away.

DRIVING through town with thousands of dollars in my possession was nerve-wracking to say the least. For a moment, I worried how I might be able to explain having found the money. Then again, Tucker had known me and my family my whole life. I doubted he would think me capable of armed robbery.

When I met him at the Sherriff's Office, Tucker led me back to the office in the corner where the words, "Larry Tucker, Sherriff" were painted in gold across the glass door.

"So, what's this all about then, Emma?" Tucker asked.

I tossed the bag onto his desk. "Look what I found in the old well out on 47."

He opened the bag and peered inside cautiously. "Hey, is this the money from Chapman's? From the robbery? Where in the world did *you* get this?"

He gave me a look of utter amazement, his blue eyes scanning me with bewilderment.

"Like I said, I was over at the old well, taking some pictures. I'm working on a new brochure for Old Fort Days, and trying to highlight some of the local landmarks." It was a lie, but I couldn't very well tell him I was the investigative proxy of the ghost of the murdered Melody Campbell. "Anyway, I pulled up the bucket to take some snapshots with it on the edge of the well, and when I did, I found this."

"Wow. I mean, just...wow. I can't believe it." He shook his head.

"Well, I figured whoever robbed the store must've known you and your deputies were hot on their trail, and ditched the money just to be safe. Don't you think?" I gave him a coquettish look. I didn't mean to play games with him, but he was never going to put two-and-two together on his own.

Tucker leaned back in his office chair, taking off his hat and running his fingers through his thick, blonde hair. "Well, that makes sense. We haven't released this to the public yet, but we were pretty close to an arrest, ya know. I mean, you can't go around committing crimes in *our* town without the law being on your case." He folded his hands behind his head in a satisfied posture.

"Oh, of course not! Whoever did it clearly didn't realize who they were up against committing a crime around here." I smiled.

"Thanks for turning this evidence in, Emma." Tucker stood from behind his desk, and stepped around to pat my shoulder with his enormous hand. As he stood beside me, towering over me, I had to wonder how he hadn't been picked up by some pro football team based on sheer size alone.

"I'm glad I could be of help, Tucker. As soon as I saw it, I knew I had to bring it to you. I hope it helps you catch whoever you're after."

* * *

I HEADED BACK to the farm. As I drove home, I turned over the discovery in my mind. The robber had hidden the stolen money in the well, waiting for the heat to be off of them.

They had known that the old well was rarely used, but didn't count on the fact that the entrance booth for the Flower Festival, together with its security cameras, would soon be set up so close to the well's location, preventing them from feeling safe returning to retrieve the money.

Mel must've seen the person hiding something in the well from her house. When the robber saw the banner at the auction, they recognized what they were looking at – themselves, caught in the act – and assumed Melody had painted it – that it had been Melody who saw them hiding the money. They had killed her to protect their secret.

I had a lot more information than before, but I still had to figure out who was responsible for both the robbery and Melody's murder. Thinking back to the auction, I remembered that someone else, besides Lisa and me, was bidding on the banner too, but I couldn't remember who. Maybe Mayor Bigsby would remember. I decided to find him at the last day of the festival, which was the following day, and see if he could identify the third bidder. If he could, he might also be unknowingly helping me unmask Melody's murderer.

CHAPTER 15

There were some farm chores that couldn't wait, no matter what. Animals had to be fed and watered every single day. With it being Sunday, though, and the last day of the festival, Grandma, Grandpa and I decided to divide and conquer so we could get changed and make it to town early enough to enjoy the parade and all the day's festivities.

The Flower Festival Parade wound through Main Street, ending at Founder's Park, with the parade making its way through Hollow Heights Gardens and ending up in the open field that was used as the event grounds. It was the same place where the food trucks had been set up the week before, but on this day, there was a grandstand from which the winners of prizes for individual flowers would be awarded. The announcements for both the business and residential beautification awards would be announced as well.

We parked at the far end of Main Street in front of the shops, and walked up to the area where everyone was gathered near the park entrance.

"Emma!" I heard someone calling my name from the

crowd, and excused myself to Grandma and Grandpa to go find its source, which I knew had to be Suzy.

"There you are! I haven't heard from you in like two days! Is everything okay?" she asked.

"Oh, yeah, I'm fine! Sorry – just had a lot on my mind," I said.

"I bet you have," she said coyly, arching an eyebrow at me.

"What's that supposed to mean?" I asked.

"It means tell me all about your date with Billy!" Her tone was demanding and impatient. Same old Suzy – bossy as ever.

"Oh! It wasn't a *date* we just went to a dinner together. Billy was great! His speech was amazing, and everyone congratulated him on his award," I said.

"Huh." She crossed her arms, seeming annoyed. "So...that was it?"

"Yeah...what else would there be?" I lifted my shoulders as I asked the question.

"You two are so stinkin' annoying, you know that? I mean, you really don't see it, do you?" she said demandingly.

"I don't know what you're on about, but I have some big news to tell you about. You'll never believe what happened yesterday!"

I pulled her aside to the edge of the crowd, hoping no one would overhear.

"I found the money – the money from the robbery? It was in the old well at the back side of the gardens," I whispered.

"No way!" Suzy exclaimed. "How in the world did you find it?"

"We were coming back from Springfield, and had to take the back way," I started.

"Because of the chicken truck," Suzy offered. You had to love a small town – everyone knew everything that happened if it was even remotely out of the ordinary.

"Exactly! Anyway, when I saw the old well, it hit me – that's what was in the painting – the banner I bought for Grandma. Someone stole it and burned it because they didn't want anyone to see the scene of them hiding the money in the well!"

"Shut up! Emma, that's brilliant! So, who did it?" Suzy asked.

"Well, I'm still not sure. I mean, they wanted to cover up the robbery so they killed Melody because she painted the banner. Except...she *didn't* paint it. Her granddaughter, Mel, did. She uses her grandmother's last name as her artist's name sometimes. She's proud of being her namesake, so it's sort of like using a pen name for her. Lots of artists do it," I said.

"Wow," Suzy thought distractedly for a moment. "Wow! So, Emma, whoever robbed the store killed Melody and stole your banner. So what did you do with the cash?"

"I met Tucker at the Sherriff's office last night and turned it in," I said. "He still has no clue who the robber is, but at least the Chapmans will get their money back."

"Emma...isn't this all a bit, I don't know, dangerous? I mean, what if the killer realizes you've figured it out?" Suzy's eyes filled with concern.

"I still think it has to be either Dr. Langston, Cadence, or Jennie and/or Dylan. All three of them could've used the money from the robbery, and all three had a grudge against Melody. Although, the more I think about it, I don't think Dr. Langston is an armed robber, or a murderer, for that matter. It doesn't match up with what we know of him. The time I overheard him talking about *taking care of* the problem with Melody, he might have meant he'd gotten a lawyer to deal with the lawsuit or something like that. So I guess that leaves Jennie, Dylan and Cadence," I said.

"What happens now?" Suzy asked.

"Well, I'm going to see if I can draw out the killer. Maybe I can use my phone to catch them going back to the well to find the money. The ticket booth next to the field will be taken down this afternoon, so they should think the coast is finally clear," I said.

I spent a few more minutes talking to Suzy as the parade wrapped up. I knew that the town elders would all be at the grandstand, and I thought I might be able to catch Mayor Bigsby. He would be in re-election mode, smiling and shaking hands with everyone, so getting a few minutes with him to ask about the other bidder at the auction might be easier than usual.

I made my way through the crowd, and saw Mayor Bigsby at the back of the grandstand with Betty Blackwood, and a few other prominent townsfolk.

"Mayor Bigsby!" I said enthusiastically. "I was wondering if I could steal a moment of your time?"

"Hello, Emma! I would love to, but I'm quite busy at the moment, as you see. Could we maybe schedule some time later in the week?" He kept his politician's smile as we spoke, giving me an idea.

"Oh, you know what? Someone told me you wouldn't be able to spare even five minutes for me today, but I told them, 'Mayor Bigsby always has time for his constituents!' Isn't that right?" I gave him a doe-eyed smile, and he laughed nervously.

"You...are so right, of course! I can spare five minutes. How can I help?" He put a hand on my shoulder and guided me to the edge of the busy area.

"I know this seems like such a small thing, but I don't suppose you remember who was the other person bidding on Melody's banner at the auction the other day, do you? Lisa Teller-Parks and I were in a bit of a bidding war, but someone else was bidding on it as well...I just can't remember who," I said.

"Well, now Emma, that's a bit of an odd question...let me think. It was Melody's banner, you say? Rest her soul!" He looked up as he said the last phrase.

"Yes, it was hers. You see, someone stole it from our front porch, and my Grandma is devastated. I thought maybe whoever was bidding might have some of Melody's work from previous years, and be willing to sell me a piece as a replacement for my poor Grandma." It was a complete lie, but I thought I sounded pretty convincing.

"Well, let's see...that was the second item, I think. So if I remember right, it was you, Lisa, and I think Cadence Campbell was the third bidder, but she dropped out pretty early. I think that little rivalry between you and Lisa got too rich for her blood, you know?" He chuckled.

Cadence! Of course! I realized at once exactly what had happened, and knew I had to go check out Cadence's place while she was still at the festival.

"Thanks so much, Mayor Bigsby! I appreciate the help!" I quickly excused myself.

"You're most welcome, Emma! And I hope I can count on your support next term!" I heard him call as I made my way across the festival grounds.

CHAPTER 16

I wasted no time jumping in the farm truck and heading out to the cemetery. When I got to the visitor center, the back of which was Cadence's home, it was empty. Just as I had suspected, Cadence, like everyone else in town, was enjoying the festivities. I thought for a moment about what Billy had said. Breaking and entering was certainly not an ideal way to collect evidence, but in the grand scheme of things, how bad was it really if it helped me catch a murderer?

I went to the back of the building and, after a brief search, found a spare key to the backdoor hidden under a flowerpot. Apparently, neither of the Campbell sisters had ever been big on security. I let myself in through the tiny kitchen, and began looking for any clues that would help prove the case of Cadence as the murderer.

Unlike the messy, bohemian space of her sister's home, Cadence's place was neat as a pin. The countertops were free from clutter, and the efficiency stove was so clean it shone. I walked through to the next room which, had it been in New York, would have been described as a bed-sit. It had a small, twin daybed on one wall which was neatly made up with a few throw pillows along the back so that it could double as a sofa. There was a small glider-rocker in the corner, and an ancient-looking wardrobe on the opposite wall. In front of the daybed was a flat-top steamer trunk which seemed to serve dual-duty as a coffee table. Although each piece was weathered and worn, everything was clean and neat.

I stood over the coffee table and looked around the room again, hoping something would jump out at me as some sort of clue. I was about to walk out when a flash of color caught my eye at the corner of the daybed. I carefully lifted the corner of the mattress to find a blue envelope tucked there. I removed the large envelope from its hiding place, and opened it carefully. When I tipped it up, a handful of travel brochures and printed pages fell out onto the coffee table.

Visit Brazil, one brochure urged, while another talked about the *perfect weather and friendly people.* The printed pages included information on buying property and opening bank accounts as an American ex-patriate.

Of course, I thought. *No extradition treaty – the great train robbery bandits had escaped to Brazil and never been brought to justice,* I remembered.

So, it seemed that Cadence's plan had been to take the money and flee the country. I put the brochures back in their hiding place, and looked around the room again. Though I was against crime in general, I could understand Cadence's desperation. The room alluded to a miserable, meager existence.

Deciding I had better get out of there and set the rest of my plan in motion, I quickly exited out the back door. After locking up, I returned the key to its hiding spot, and walked back to the truck, which I had parked among the headstones so that any passerby might mistake me for a visitor.

I headed back to town and parked the truck in the same

spot where we had left it before. I had some work to do before I met back up with Grandma and Grandpa. If I was going to get Cadence to confess, she had to believe that there was something at stake. I looked for Suzy or Brian as I made my way through the festival grounds. As I pushed through the crowd toward the grandstand, I heard a familiar laugh. *Suzy!* I followed the sound, and grabbed her wrist when I found her, so I wouldn't lose her again.

"Hey, Emma! I wondered where you were!" She hugged my neck.

"Hi, Suz!" I leaned in to whisper, "I think I know who did it. We need to set her up though. Are you up for helping me?"

She nodded, and I took her hand and pulled her out of the bustle of the crowd to a quieter spot near the edge of the festival grounds.

"So, who was it?" Suzy asked as soon as we were in a place quiet enough to hear each other.

"Well, I think it was Cadence," I replied.

I told Suzy that Mayor Bigsby remembered Cadence being the other person to bid on the banner in the auction. I also told her about what I had found in Cadence's little shack. "So, I plan to find Cadence, and casually mention to you, within her earshot, that the police are close to figuring out where the money is hidden. That should make her desperate enough to take a chance. When she goes back for it, I'll catch her in the act, and get her to confess, recording the whole thing on my phone."

"That's a great plan, Emma. There's just one problem...I think it's about to be foiled." She pointed to the grandstand behind me, where Tucker was walking up to the microphone.

No, no, no! Tucker, please don't mention the money...you have no idea what you're about to do! My inner voice pleaded, but as soon as he opened his mouth, I knew what he was about to say.

"Ladies and gentlemen, I have an announcement," Tucker began, leaning over to get his tall frame close enough to the microphone to be heard. "We made a breakthrough in the robbery of Chapman's store last night. A good Samaritan found the missing money, and returned it to the Sherriff's department. That money will be returned to its rightful owners." The crowd cheered in response. "We are, of course, still looking for the perpetrator of the robbery. If you have any information about the robbery at Chapman's store, please contact the Sherriff's department right away. Thank you. Have fun, and be safe, everybody!" He waved a giant palm in the air on the last word.

"Are you kidding me right now?" I heaved a sigh as the words left my lips.

"No, it's okay! I have an idea!" Suzy pointed to a floppy hat in the crowd. "There's Cadence. Come with me, and follow my lead."

I was hoping that her bossiness was going to come in handy for a change.

Suzy stood right behind Cadence and started talking to me loudly. "So, Emma," her voice was exaggerated, and I kept an eye on Cadence's body language. "I saw you dancing with Tucker the other night. You two seem pretty chummy to me. Did he tell you anything about who they think the robber might be?" She winked at me as she said the last words. Cadence's body tensed visibly.

"Oh, that!" I laughed. "He did mention that they were getting close to catching the suspect."

"Really?! Did he tell you who they thought did it? Come on, you can tell me – I won't tell a soul!" Suzy was really getting into acting out our little skit.

"No, but he did say...oh, I don't know if I should share." I feigned hesitation. I could see Cadence turning her head a little, as if trying to hear us more clearly. At that moment, I realized that we had also captured the attention of another nearby festival-goer. Jennie Weaver stood just a few people down from Cadence with her boyfriend Dylan.

"Come on, Emma! I tell you everything," Suzy added to our conversation for authenticity.

"Well, okay, if you promise not to say anything. He said that there was some big piece of evidence in the same place where the money was found," I said, hoping I sounded convincing.

"Oh really? Where is that?" she asked.

"Oh, I can't tell you that! Even I'm not one-hundred-percent sure. But Tucker said that they were going to go back over there early in the morning to 'process the scene' or something. I don't understand all that technical police talk, really. Anyway, he is sure whatever this piece of evidence is, will put the culprit away for a long, long time!"

At that, Cadence began to shift back and forth, and look around nervously.

"Hey, off topic, but what time does the entrance booth down on 47 shut down? I'm sick of the traffic over there!" I winced a little as I said it, knowing I wasn't being as subtle as I'd like.

"It's supposed to be closed at sundown, from what I hear. When the fireworks show starts, it's the end of the festival," Suzy responded.

We walked off toward the ice cream stand, and I kept an eye on both Cadence and Jennie as long as I could.

"You did great, Suz," I told her.

I saw Jennie tugging Dylan by the arm, and leading him out of the festival grounds, back toward Main Street. While I had my eyes on them, Cadence disappeared into the crowd.

"Thanks! I always thought I should do community

theater!" Suzy said, flipping her blonde hair back over her shoulder theatrically. We both laughed.

"Did you see Jennie Weaver was standing near us as well?" I asked.

"Do you suppose she heard us?" Suzy replied.

"I think she had to have – everyone around could've heard us, we were so loud," I replied.

"So, do you want me to come with you to confront the killer?"

"No, I'll be fine," I replied. Suzy grabbed her phone and started typing. "What are you doing?" I asked.

"Texting Billy. If you don't want me to come with you, he should. If one of them really did rob the store at gunpoint, not to mention kill Melody, she won't hesitate to hurt you. I won't let you take the risk alone," Suzy replied.

I didn't know why, but something told me if I was going to pull this plan off, it had to be on my own. I grasped Suzy's wrist in my hand. "No, Suzy. I've got this. Trust me – if I get into any trouble, I'll call for help. I'm tougher than I look, ya know," I said, playfully flexing my arm.

"Uh, well, you'd have to be!" Suzy laughed. "But seriously, if you get into any trouble, just say the word and I'll come runnin!"

CHAPTER 17

*a*fter I left Suzy, I found Grandma and Grandpa, who were, luckily for me, ready to leave.

As we pulled into the driveway at home, I pretended to get a text from Suzy asking if I could come back down and help her at the shop for a couple of hours. After Grandma and Grandpa got out, I turned the truck around and headed down to the old well.

The part of County Road 47 nearest the back entrance to Hollow Heights Gardens was peppered with houses and the odd business, like Lisa Marie's Salon, a hair salon operating out of what had previously been a small home. There were open lots too, though, and areas of overgrown brush. Just before the clearing where the old well stood was an overgrown patch of trees and bushes.

I carefully pulled the truck far enough into the bushes to conceal it, and walked over to a spot that gave me a clear view of the well, the entrance to the park, and the highway.

It was starting to get dark, and the person manning the booth by the back park entrance had gone. As the sky grew dim, I heard a pop overhead, and looked up to see the first of the evening fireworks. If Cadence was the killer, she should show up at any moment.

I sat a little while longer, trying not to get distracted by the explosions of color and sound overhead. Just when I was beginning to worry I had gotten it all wrong, an old white and silver pickup truck pulled into the parking spot next to the empty ticket booth. The driver killed the lights, and I heard the heavy door of the pickup creak open and slam shut. I peered through the trees and soon saw a small, dark figure approaching the well, carrying a pocket flashlight. The small beam of light danced in the tall grass, then circled the well.

The figure paced back and forth in the weeds for several minutes examining the ground, looking for some unseen object. It was definitely someone small – probably a woman. It could have been Jennie or Cadence. I simply couldn't tell in the dark. The slender figure leaned into the well, the light from the flashlight disappearing into the dark abyss. The figure turned again, scanning back and forth against the far side of the clearing, almost reaching the tree line when I heard a sound that made me freeze and hold my breath. It was the familiar *swoosh* of an incoming text message.

I looked down at my phone, fumbling madly for the buttons on the side to silence it, but instead, another text arrived, and with it, the offending swoosh repeated.

I looked up and saw the figure moving quickly across the field toward me. As it came closer, I recognized it to be the very person I suspected might show up. Cadence Campbell.

"Who's back there?" I heard the raspy voice call out. "I'm not afraid of you. I've got a gun and I know how to use it!" she said, louder.

I know you do, I thought.

I backed up a little, hoping to make it as far as my truck,

but I stumbled on a branch and tripped, careening backward onto the forest floor. I stifled a yelp, but was sure the ruckus had caught Cadence's attention. I tried to move back further on my hands and feet, reminding myself of the crab soccer game we used to play at school. Suddenly my mind flashed to playing the game in the middle school gym with Suzy and Billy. Was this going to be the end for me? Was I ever going to see them again?

I tumbled over and scrambled to my feet. The sounds of leaves and twigs being crushed underfoot, getting closer and closer sent my heart to my throat. They say that in moments of fear, each person exhibits one of two responses: fight or flight. This was a moment of fear if I had ever had one. It was time to see what I was really made of.

"Come on out now, and I won't hurt you," Cadence said as she grew closer.

"That sounds like a lie to me," I replied boldly. *Okay, Emma. Fight it is,* I thought.

"Who is that? Who's talking?" she replied.

"Who me?" I backed up a bit more, and moved to my right, finding my way further into the thicket of trees. "I'm just the woman who is going to send you to prison, that's all."

"What are you saying? I've done nothing wrong!" she said, her voice cracking a bit.

"That's not what I hear, Cadence." I took several fast steps to the right, trying to throw her off of my location. "I hear you knocked over Chapman's store."

"An old woman like me? So frail? They say I'm crazy too, ya know. The odd bird in town. My sister – she was the *eccentric* one. They call you eccentric when you have a nice house and a big talent. When you're talentless and poor, though, they just call ya crazy!" She was growing angry, the years of pent up bitterness finally bubbling to the surface.

"Oh? Is that why you killed Melody? Because she was the

talented one?" I was taunting her a little, but hoped it would buy me some time.

"She wasn't the only talented one, ya know! I had the most beautiful singing voice! I could've done something with my life, but oh, no! Melody wouldn't have it! Every time I talked about leaving, she would cry and wail, and carry on! She was so afraid of being left all alone. I could've gone to Branson and starred in one of the reviews. Maybe Nashville, even! But *she* wouldn't let me go!" Cadence's voice was full of hate and venom.

"Let's talk about it, Cadence. Put the gun down and come on out into the clearing. You can tell me all about it. I know she hurt you, Cadence. I know she took the man you wanted." I softened my voice, trying to appeal to her by leveraging that hurt that I knew lingered deep inside.

The woods grew quiet for a moment, and I couldn't quite tell where Cadence was. I listened intently, then I heard it. Sobbing. Cadence was crying. Maybe I had gotten to her after all. I slowly started to move forward, then I heard the sobbing turn into a wail. "She took everything from me! She took my home and my future and the only man I ever loved! She deserved what she got!" Cadence was moving fast then, tromping through the woods in my direction.

I moved quickly, zig-zagging back and forth to keep her off my trail as best I could, but she was gaining on me. I remembered my phone was in my hand, and I tried to dial, but had no signal. *Sugar!* I decided to do the only thing I could. If Cadence was going to do me in, at least I could record my own demise. I hit the video record button on my phone and stuck it in my pocket, microphone side out.

As Cadence saw me in the woods, I moved quickly to my right and into the edge of the clearing. She stepped out from the trees slowly, the tiny revolver in her hand pointed at me from waist level.

"Now Cadence, listen, I'm on your side! Why don't you tell me what happened? I'm sure it was all just a big mistake," I lied, hoping to at least buy myself some time.

"What happened? Oh, I think you know what happened, Hooper girl," she hissed.

"Well, if this is it, let's at least start at the beginning. Why did you rob Chapman's?"

"Don't you know? I mean, someone was in my house. I'm guessing that was you, wasn't it? Things were out of place. I don't leave things out of place, so I knew someone had been there." She stepped forward, and I stepped back, hands up.

"I just wanted to talk to you, but you weren't home," I replied.

"Bah! You were snooping, that's what you were doing. Hooper the snooper! That's what you are!" she said, taking another step forward.

"Okay, you got me. But now is your chance to get it all off your chest. Why Chapman's? What had they done to you?" I asked trying to feign as much empathy as I could while I thought of any possible way out of my current predicament.

"Oh, nothing – nothing at all! I just needed the money. I was sick of living in that little tumbledown shack. Tired of spending my days digging holes and cleaning headstones. It's not much of a life if you spend every day among the dead, you know." She chuckled to herself.

"And so you must've thought that Tucker was onto you – and decided to hide the money here, but then the ticket booth went up," I pointed toward the little structure across the road, "and you had to wait to come back for it."

"Hmm, you are pretty clever after all. Shame you're not going to live long enough to put that pretty face and big brain to use."

"So what about the banner – did you take it from our house?" I asked.

"I did. Ya see, I tried to buy it that day at the auction, but you and Lisa were so bound and determined to outdo each other...ironic, really. Kind of like me and Melody. Except, Melody always outdid me in everything. That's why she had to go, don't ya see? She was always rubbing my failures in my face. I knew when I saw that banner that she had seen me hiding the money. I couldn't let her hang that over my head, so I was going to follow her out to her place – tell her I planned on getting outta her hair once and for all..." She trailed off as if she were replaying the scene in her mind.

"But you saw her on the side of the road and you took advantage of the fact that no one was around," I speculated.

"I saw her walking along the side of the road, and she turned around just a little – not enough to see me, but just a little. It took me back to that day...that awful day so long ago." She had the wistful look again. I almost felt sorry for her, but I couldn't forget she had a gun.

"What day?" I asked.

"The day I learned she had stolen the man I wanted...she was so smug...so superior. There was never anything for me with Melody around. I was barely a year old when she was born, and she sucked the life out of everything I had ever since." She shook her head, and I thought I saw a tear rolling down her cheek in the moonlight.

I tried to take a few steps, but the dry leaves underfoot betrayed me, and she returned her attention to me. "So what happened to the man, Cadence? The one both you and Melody loved?"

"That's the sad thing. She didn't even want him. He wanted to marry her but she said she wanted to raise their baby on her own. Can you imagine what that would have been like for me? Having him coming around every Christmas and birthday, the man I loved, making eyes at my sister, who didn't even want him? I couldn't have that. No, that wouldn't do at all." She shook her head as if she were saying the most reasonable thing in the world.

"What happened to him, Cadence?" I asked again, already suspecting the answer.

"I snuck into his place and put a bullet in him. Then I rolled him up in a blanket, put him in a wheelbarrow, and dumped him right into the Mississippi River. I'll never forget the sound he made when he went into the water. Nobody ever learned what happened to him. After that, I moved out of Melody's place, took the cemetery caretaker's job, and have been in that lousy cabin ever since. I thought if I could get a little money together, I could start over. I'm only sixty. Don't I have some livin' left to do? Don't I deserve a chance to be happy?" She was weeping, then rubbing her eyes with the back of her hand.

"So you saw the banner, and you thought..." I started but she interrupted me.

"I *knew* that the hateful cow was mockin' me! She saw me hide the money, and when I was goin' down to tell her I'd be out of her hair soon enough, I saw her walkin', and she turned back... and I just sort of veered off the road and the next thing I knew, I was back at home, sprayin' off the front of my truck with the hose."

Cadence hesitated, then continued. "I had to be sure she didn't leave any notes or evidence behind. She had a big mouth, my sister, and liked to write everything down, ya know. But I looked high and low in her house and didn't find a thing. I snuck up to your place, took the banner off the front porch and burned it. I'm sorry about that – your Grandma is a good woman – but I had to be sure nobody would see it and put two and two together." Cadence looked dazed, the emotion of the confession clearly beginning to wear on her.

If I'm careful, I thought, *I can get her to give me the gun.* I took a few steps forward.

"Give me the gun, Cadence. Let's go talk to Tucker and work this all out. You didn't mean to kill Melody, did you? You just sort of blacked out. Let's go see Tucker – he can help us." I stepped closer, one hand raised, the other reaching out, palm open, trying to get her to give me the gun.

"No, no. I'm a two-time loser. I might as well make it three." She waved the gun around in the air before pointing it loosely in my direction.

"It was all a mistake, Cadence. It wasn't even Melody who painted the banner." I was blathering on, trying anything to get her to see some sort of reason. But I knew immediately it had been the wrong thing to say.

"What? What do you mean?" Her demeanor spun on a dime, going from resigned and sad to filled with fury. "Tell me!" She shook the gun at me again.

"It-it was Mel – her granddaughter. She painted it," I blurted out. *What have I done? If she shoots me, she might go hurt Mel too!*

She turned away from me, slowly, looking across the road to the little house on the corner where one light was on in the back bedroom. I knew just whose bedroom that had to be, and I had to stop Cadence from getting to her. As Cadence's pace quickened, I walked quickly behind her, and lunged to grab the gun from her hand.

I missed, knocking her to the ground, but the gun went flying. I couldn't see where it went, but it looked like Cadence couldn't either. She stood up and ran toward me, hands outstretched. I ducked my head and came back at her, using a move I had seen in college football. It might have worked well for a three-hundred pound lineman, but at five-two and a buck-twenty, it wasn't so effective for me.

We grappled back and forth, and she rolled on top of me, her hands wrapping around my throat. *She's twice my age – how is she this strong?* I wondered.

I tried to kick at her back with my feet, and rocked back and forth trying to free my neck from her grip, but I was getting nowhere. Suddenly she turned, and looked back toward the woods. She loosened her grip enough for me to breathe, but not enough for me to get away from her.

"Did you hear that?" she asked, her eyes transfixed on the woods.

"Hear...what..." my voice croaked under the strain of her grip.

"That...that...voice..." She cocked her head to the side, as if trying to hear it more distinctly.

I listened to see if I could make out what she meant. I had hoped it was Tucker, Suzy, Billy – anybody who could get this madwoman off of me. Suddenly, I heard what she meant. The sound was soft, as if being carried to us from a faraway place on the wind. *Cadence* I heard the voice say faintly.

She freed my neck, standing up. "Who's there? It can't be you. It's not. It can't be!" She stood, frozen, the blood draining from her face as she looked into the distance, and the call came again. *Caaa-deeeence.*

I jumped up and started looking around to see if I could find the gun. I couldn't be sure but if the ethereal voice was who I thought it was, maybe I was getting some help of the supernatural kind.

Looking up, I saw Cadence backing away from the woods. "No...no! No! I killed you...you can't be here. You're not real. Leave me alone!" She was pale, her voice high and shrieking as she continued to back up toward the middle of the clearing.

Caaa-deeeence, the voice called again. Cadence continued

to step back. I saw where she was heading, and tried to stop her.

"Cadence, stop! No! You're too close!" I started toward her, but I was too late.

She shrieked – the most blood-curdling sound I had ever heard. I turned in the direction of her gaze and saw the figure with whom I had become so familiar in the recent days. I looked back to Cadence just in time to see her tumbling backward over the edge of the well.

I ran to the spot from which she had fallen, and by the time I got there, her screams had stopped. The old well was dry and hundreds of feet deep. She could never have survived the fall.

I turned back to where Melody was floating just inches above the ground. She wasn't smirking this time, nor did she have anything clever to say. Instead, there were lines from her eyes down to her chin that looked like a blur. *Ghostly tears,* I thought.

"I'm so sorry, Melody. I wish it hadn't been her," I said.

She nodded her head gently up and down, then moved past me and descended into the well to join her sister.

I ran my fingers through my hair. I would have to walk across to one of the houses to get someone to call the police. Not Kayla's though. I pulled my phone from my pocket. It had four bars of service. I couldn't help but wonder if Melody had anything to do with my lack of service earlier. Maybe she was there the whole time. Maybe she needed to hear everything in order to understand it all for herself.

* * *

TUCKER CAME and took my statement. "You sure have a knack for being in the wrong place at the wrong time,

Emma," he said, shaking his head. "You want me to call Dr. Will to come check you out?"

"Not a chance, Tuck." I shook my head. "I'm fine, and don't need the lecture. Not tonight, anyway."

CHAPTER 18

*J*took it easy the next day, sleeping in and foregoing my chores. Neither Grandma nor Grandpa was bothered in the least by my sudden-onset idleness. I spent the morning doing some work online, and getting things lined up to go get the rest of my things from New York. After everything that had happened in the past few weeks, I knew I wasn't going back. That was the thing about Hillbilly Hollow. It wasn't a big, shiny kind of place, but somehow it pulled you in. It was the people, I realized, that made the place so special. Sure, some had their problems, but wasn't that the case anywhere you went? No, I was glad I had gone off to the city and had my adventures when I was younger, but I was happy to be home.

I gave Snowball a much-needed bath when I woke up. I had arranged to stop by the dentist's office in town. Dr. Parker had purchased several of Melody's banners in years past, and had several other pieces of her work. Dr. Parker had agreed to sell me his banner from the prior year's Flower Festival.

147

"I heard what happened, Emma," Dr. Parker had said when I came into his office.

"Yeah, it was all pretty crazy," I replied. "I'm still sort of trying to process it all, really."

"I bet," he said. "I'm glad you called. I'm happy to help you out. Here's the banner," he said, pulling a carefully wrapped package from the bottom drawer of his desk. He gently unfolded the banner, which depicted sprays of flowers in Melody's classic impressionist-cubist style. The colors were vibrant and overall the piece had a happy feeling about it.

I hadn't liked Melody's work at first, but it had definitely grown on me. I couldn't help but wonder if Mel would continue painting in her grandmother's style, and if she would keep using her artist's name of Campbell. I lightly touched the fabric of the banner laid across Dr. Parker's desk.

"It's beautiful," I told him. "Thank you so much for being willing to part with it. I know my Grandma will be ecstatic." I smiled.

"She's a fine lady, your grandmother. I've known her most of my life," he said. Dr. Parker was older than me, but not quite as old as my grandparents.

"She really is something else," I said. "Thanks again," I said as I left.

When I got back to the farm, I had Grandma help me hang the banner on the front porch where the previous one had been.

"I love it, Emma," Grandma said when she stood back and looked at it. "I really do just love it. I've always wanted one of Melody's paintings. I can't believe I finally have one." She hugged me and kissed me on the cheek.

"I'm glad you like it, Grandma. I think this one is even nicer than the first one." I smiled.

I puttered around in the garden a bit with Grandma in

the afternoon, picking strawberries and then we walked down to the stand of fruit trees at the edge of the property and pulled some peaches to can.

I felt a little more energetic in the afternoon, and decided to bake a butter cake that I thought we could have with dinner. I decided that it would also be nice to go for a little walk and maybe read a book. I grabbed a blanket and a thermos of iced tea and headed for the hill at the top of the meadow. It was my favorite spot on the farm, especially in the late afternoon when the sun shone down golden on the green earth below.

As I walked up the path to the top of the hill with Snowball by my side I felt content and happy. My phone buzzed in my pocket. It was a text from Billy.

BILLY: Come 2 dinner 2night?

ME: Rather stay home. U come eat with us. Grandmas making chicken.

BILLY: On my way!

WHEN I GOT to the top of the meadow, I spread out the blanket and settled down with my book, propping myself up on my elbows. Snowball curled up by my side, and I was glad I had given her a bath when she snuggled into my leg. I lay there, reading leisurely for a while, until I heard movement in the grass ahead of me. I looked up to see Billy standing over me.

"I thought I might find you up here," he said. "It was always one of our favorite spots." He smiled down at me, shielding his eyes from the setting sun.

"Still is," I said, flipping over to sit upright. I patted the blanket beside me. "Join me?" Billy plopped down on the blanket next to me, eliciting a bleat from Snowball.

"So, how are you feeling?" he asked.

"Pretty good, actually. I'm sorry about what happened with Cadence, obviously, but with everything she told me... she was really troubled," I said.

"Now Emma, you know you couldn't have done anything to save her." He put his arm around my shoulders and half-hugged me.

"I know. It's just sad," I replied.

"Any more sightings of Melody since the well?" he asked.

"No, and I don't think I'll see her again. Now that we know what happened, I think she's probably at rest," I said. "But then again, based on what Dr. Edelson said, that doesn't mean that I won't see someone else sometime. And if I do, that's okay, but if I don't, that's okay too. I wouldn't be so at ease about it all if it wasn't for you introducing me to him, you know. Thanks for that." I patted his knee.

"I'm glad I could help," Billy replied. "Should we start heading back to the house? I'm not going to lie – I drove extra fast when you said Grandma Hooper was making chicken." He chuckled and stood up, reaching for my hand to pull me up.

In that moment, something suddenly felt different. Billy held my hand in his as we stood there in one of our favorite spots from childhood. I felt transported back to our youth when I sat with Billy on this hillside dozens of times hoping he would hold my hand, or better yet, kiss me, and yet, it never happened. Now, he was holding my hand and looking down at me sweetly as we stood on the hillside at sunset. I couldn't help but feel like he was going to kiss me, and I wasn't sure how I felt about it. We had always flirted a little but he was my best friend. I wasn't sure if moving to romance would be worth the risk. As Billy leaned forward and put his hands on my shoulders, his phone buzzed.

Saved by the bell, I thought.

He pulled his phone from his pocket and looked at it.

"Uh-oh," he said. "I'm afraid I'll have to take a raincheck on that chicken, Emma." He leaned down and scooped up the blanket, handing it to me along with my book. "That's a text from Tucker. There's been some kind of accident. They need me in town."

I suddenly got a cold chill.

He shook his head, and led me back down the trail toward the house. "Save me a butter bar?" he said as we got to the house. "I'll talk to you later. Goodnight, Emma." He winked at me, got in his truck, and drove back down the driveway.

As I walked into the house, I thought about what we had talked about. I wondered who needed Billy, and if he would be able to help them. One thing that I felt pretty certain of, though, was that I may have seen the last of Melody Campbell, but I felt sure that I would be visited by spirits again. I wasn't sure when, or who, but I would do my best to help them if I could. I felt a newfound peace, and knew that, if I could help someone else find peace too, I would.

Continue following the ghostly mysteries and eccentric characters of Hillbilly Hollow in
"A Dastardly Death in Hillbilly Hollow"

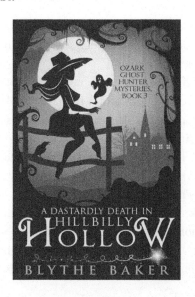

After Billy left, I sat for a while and thought about Prudence. I couldn't believe she would go so far as to try and take her own life.

She may not have found the love she was looking for, and I knew she had been really down when Preacher Jacob had spurned her advances and then died before she could try to change his mind. Still, she loved playing the organ at the church. She volunteered for several local charities, and was secretary of the Mount Olivet Church Historical Preservation Society. She had worked tirelessly to get the building on the Missouri list of registered historic places, and had finally succeeded. The early nineteenth century building was finally going to receive its official plaque, and be listed on the state guide to historic places. Now, it looked like she might not live to see her work come to fruition.

After tossing and turning for a while, I must have finally been so exhausted that I drifted off to sleep. It wasn't the crows that woke me the next morning, or one of Grandma's rooftop serenades. Instead, it was the sound of my normally calm sidekick, Snowball, bleating. I opened my eyes to find her on my bed, her nose inches from mine, as she bleated at the top of her little lungs. Having never awakened to the smell of goat breath, it is an experience I would highly discourage anyone from trying.

"What is your problem? And get your dirty hooves off my bed!" I gave her a nudge with my forearm and she jumped down. Still, she wouldn't stop crying. I rubbed my eyes and sat up, cross-legged in my bed. "Seriously, what is..." I stopped short when I looked at the foot of my bed.

Prudence Huffler was sitting on the edge of my bed, knees together, both palms in her lap, just as she did in church.

"Hello, Emma," Prudence said cheerfully.

I gasped. "Prudence!" I shook my head as if to make sure I was really awake. "Oh no, Prudence, no! You didn't make it?" I asked, tears starting to form in my eyes.

"Didn't make what?" Prudence asked, cocking her head to the side. When I had seen ghosts before, they had always been ethereal, diaphanous, and their appearance seemed tenuous. Prudence, though, did not look like the other spirits I had seen. She was almost translucent, but her color was vivid. She wore long-sleeved flannel pajamas with matching long pants. They were baby blue, and had a pattern of pianos all over them. Her brown hair looked the same color it always had, and the green of her eyes was a vivid emerald.

"Prudence, I don't know how to tell you this..." I had never before had to break the news to a spirit that they had passed on. I didn't know what effect it would have on her. "You were in the hospital, in a coma. You-you tried to end your life, Prudence, and if I can see you, that means, well, I'm afraid you've passed on. I'm so, so sorry!"

Prudence laughed, a small but hearty laugh with a little pig-snort at the end. Even in death the poor girl was not smooth.

"No, Emma! I'm not dead!"

"What? But....I can see you. You have to be dead," I replied, growing more confused. I wondered if she was in some sort of ghostly denial.

"No!" She waved her hand back and forth dismissively. "I'm in a coma. I was in the hospital, and everyone was making such a fuss over me. Dr. Will was there, and Tucker, and some nurses, and some doctor from the hospital was talking to Dr. Will. All of a sudden, it got really, really quiet. Then I heard a voice calling my name, so I got up and started walking toward it. I went out into the hall, and there was this bright light behind the door at the end, and that sounded like where the voice was coming from."

Prudence's story reminded me of those shows Grandma watched about people who had been to the brink of death, and lived to tell the tale.

"Anyway, as I got to the door, it sounded like my Granny Alene, but she's been dead since I was in high school, so I knew it couldn't be her. There was another hallway right before the doorway, and I walked down it instead. The next thing I knew, I was in your front yard, so I thought I'd come talk to you," Prudence said.

"Oh...okay." Most of the spirits who had visited me had a particular purpose. I wasn't sure how to make small talk with someone from the other side. "So, what did you want to talk to me about?"

"Well, when I was in my room, I heard Dr. Will say that I had taken some pills and tried to kill myself. I know you and he are close, so I wanted you to talk to him for me," she said.

"You did take pills, Prudence. You did try to kill yourself," I responded.

"No, Emma, I didn't! I would never kill myself. I don't know what happened. I remember eating steak earlier that night, then I got a phone call, and remember when I hung up

I had a terrible headache. I don't remember a thing after that until I was in the hospital," she said, shaking her head, her brow furrowed. "You've gotta help me, Emma! I can't have people thinking I hurt myself. Especially Mama – she'll be devastated!"

"Okay, Prudence. I'll see what I can do to help. I can't exactly tell people we've talked though, unless I want to end up in the loony bin. You don't remember who you were with that night? Is there someone who might try to hurt you at all?" I asked.

Her brow still furrowed and her face bearing more concern, she shook her head again. "No. I have no idea who would want to hurt me."

Suddenly, Prudence disappeared and reappeared once, then again, like the picture on a television when the power surges. "What's happening?" I asked her, unsure if she would know any more than I did.

"I don't know. I feel strange." Her expression turned to one of someone who looks like they're about to be sick. "I think I have to go back, Emma. Please, just do whatever you can to find out what happened. Don't let Mama believe a lie about me. You're the only one who can help!"

"I'll try, Prudence, I promise," I said. I started to reach out my hand to pat her arm, and realized I couldn't.

"Thank you, Emma! Thank you so –" and with that, she disappeared.

END OF EXCERPT

ABOUT THE AUTHOR

Blythe Baker is a thirty-something bottle redhead from the South Central part of the country. When she's not slinging words and creating new worlds and characters, she's acting as chauffeur to her children and head groomer to her household of beloved pets.

Blythe enjoys long walks with her dog on sweaty days, grubbing in her flower garden, cooking, and ruthlessly de-cluttering her overcrowded home. She also likes binge-watching mystery shows on TV and burying herself in books about murder.

To learn more about Blythe, visit her website and sign up for her newsletter at www.blythebaker.com

Made in the USA
Las Vegas, NV
11 February 2023